# The Beasts MC

## The Complete Collection

CU00867501

## By Mason Lee

© 2016

**The Complete Collection *The Beasts MC* series!**

"Bulldog" Williams is not your typical man. Not only is he a sexy outlaw biker, but he is also one of the most powerful werewolves to ever wear the colors of the The Beasts Motorcycle Club. He had everything a man like him could possibly want: money, power and, most of all, freedom.

The only thing that he didn't have was a way to fill the hole that was deep in his heart.

That is, until he meets Steve. Now, a chance encounter has given him a choice: to risk it all and go after the one thing that he is missing or to stay with his pack and his club.

Does he have the courage and strength to take on the greatest risk of all?

Note: Parts of *The Beasts MC* were previously published as *Outlaw Wolf.*

Also includes sneak peeks at upcoming novels!

# Volume One - The Beasts Club

"Bulldog" Williams sat on the low brick wall at the edge of the campgrounds and watched his buddies enjoy the festivities. The full moon parties were always the highlight of the month for the club. The beer was flowing, the cute twinkie boys were dancing and the bonfire was burning bright and strong.

Bulldog didn't feel much like partying tonight, however. He was getting more and more restless as the days went by and he didn't know what to do. It wasn't as if he didn't love the club and his brothers – they were his life. But he had started to wonder if maybe there was something more to life than this town and the club. He had been with them for seven years and he'd been glad to be part of it. Being with them had not only given him a sense of purpose; it had saved his life. They were his friends, his family. He could not even remember what his life had been like before he was one of the Beasts. Deep down, he didn't want to remember what life had been like before he wore the club patch on his back. He loved his life now. But there were times, times like this night, when he did wonder if there was something more out there, just waiting for him to find it.

The Beasts were a very special motorcycle club. They were not just bikers; they were a werewolf pack. Every single member of the group was a wolf. Most of them were full bloods but there were three turned wolves among them as well. The brothers didn't discriminate; they accepted the turned wolves the same as if they had been born full blood. Once you were a member of The Beasts, you were equal with every other member.

Bulldog looked over to the deck where the food and drinks were set up. It was a veritable cornucopia of food. Hot wings, brats, other sausages, grilled chicken, slider hamburgers, strip steaks and rolls, deep fried turkey legs, cups of chili, a big bowl of meat and *queso* dip and chips, grilled shrimp, crab salad and rolls, meat balls, sausage balls, and several kinds of pizza, all of which were meat topped. The unifying theme of all of the food was that it was all meat-based. That was not a coincidence. There was enough food to feed an army and yet not a single bite would be left behind in the morning. The sad part was that with all of the food that was on the deck, it would still not be enough. There was still the main course to be served, and it would be served fresh and raw. There was plenty to drink as well: cases of beer, bottles of wine, and lots of hard liquor, not to mention the five-bottle punch that was already in the bowl.

The music was pounding: classic rock with a mix of heavy metal. It seemed to make the already hot and humid June night even hotter. Bulldog looked up at the stars and got lost in them for a moment. Sometimes he wanted to be somewhere else. He didn't care where – anywhere but at that party. He had never liked the full moon parties. He had gone along with them at first, when he was a new member, and for a couple of years after, but then he started to feel that they were wrong. They just did not fit with his personality. He was always up for a party but not like these. He only attended them anymore because it was absolutely mandatory. If you were a full patch, you were not allowed to miss a full moon party unless you had a damn good reason. It wouldn't do him any good to try and come up with excuses or reasons, either. Everyone knew his objections and they would see right through them. So he just made the most of it and tried to get through them as best as he could.

"Bulldog, come on over here. Sean…it was Sean, wasn't it?" another biker asked the short, thin blond man who was sitting on his lap.

"Yeah, it's Sean" the boy replied.

"Sean was just telling me how he loves to suck cock and I asked him if he had ever sucked one while he was getting fucked by a real big one. Two at the same time. He said he hadn't. What do you think about that?"

"But I'm willing to try anything once!" Sean exclaimed. The biker on whose lap he was sitting laughed out loud at the statement.

"Well, I was telling him how having his backside stuffed with a massive hunk of man meat made sucking the other cock more fun, but he didn't believe me. We was wondering if you would give us a hand with a little experiment?"

Bulldog shook his head as he smiled and looked down at the ground. Axel used the same gimmick every time. The sad part about it was that it worked every time. And every time, Bulldog just went along with it. He knew that if he didn't give in they would just continue to annoy him until he did. That was the price he paid for being special, he supposed. He finished off his beer and tossed the bottle into the trash bag nearby before standing up and walking over to where Axel and the boy were sitting on a fallen log.

"Sure, why not?" He said as he took hold of Sean's chin and moved his face up to look into his eyes. Sean was good looking. Nice eyes, healthy skin. Bulldog thought that he must have came from a good family. He didn't know what had led him to be here in their camp tonight. He had no idea why he would have come all this way to party with a bunch of dirty, rude bikers, but then, he never understood why any of them did. There was just something about the crew that drew people into it, he figured.

There were always three or four boys and a couple of girls that they managed to gather together for their monthly parties. They found them at truck stops and at the bus station, pool halls and dive bars. There was a seemingly endless supply of young men who were out on the road and using their bodies to get by. Some of them were runaways, some were hitchhikers, and some were just transients. It was always easy to spot the ones who were willing to party. This was especially true with the gay boys, as they stood out in the conservative environment of Jonesboro. The most important consideration was that they were willing to party long and party hard. He felt bad that Sean had made the choice to come to the camp that night. As he looked into Sean's eyes, he thought that it was a shame – he looked too nice to be here. All of the members of the Beasts were what you might call omnisexual. They didn't care what kind of hole they were fucking, as long as it was hot and tight. Sean would seem to fit that bill perfectly.

"What do think, Sean – you like Bulldog here? Think he can help us out with our experiment?" Axel asked.

"I don't know. I mean, he's cute and all, but does he have what it takes for us to know if this experiment is real or not?" Sean asked.

Bulldog knew where this was going and he knew that he had exactly what it took. He opened his belt and pulled open the button fly of his grimy blue jeans. He pulled the front of his dingy, sweaty jockstrap aside and hauled out his thick slab of man meat. Sean's eyes grew wide as he looked at the largest cock he had ever seen in his life, and suddenly realized that it was bigger soft even than anything he had ever seen on the most well-endowed porn stars when they were fully hard.

"Oh, my God! You're huge. It's a fucking anaconda!" The boy started to reach out his hand toward the giant piece of tube steak. He stopped short, realizing that he'd better ask the guy first for fear of overstepping his boundaries or something. "May I touch it?"

Bulldog nodded affirmatively and Sean reached out and wrapped his warm hand around the nine-inch long, three-inch wide hunk of flaccid uncut cock. The sheer heat of it was enough to indicate that the guy whose fly it was hanging out of meant business. The weight of it was suggestive and Sean's hole began to twitch in anticipation of how good it would feel to have it inside him.

"So you like that, do you, Sean?" asked Axel.

"God, yes. He's incredible!" Sean replied.

"Let's go over to the shed, guys. There's a little more privacy there," Axel said.

Bulldog stuffed his massive tool back into his pants but didn't bother to fasten them completely. The three men walked to the tool shed that stood a few yards away, tucked into the edge of the encampment. Once they were inside, the two bikers wasted little time pulling off Sean's shirt and slipping his jeans down his legs. He was wearing a pair of lime green and hot pink trimmed swim trunks underneath. It looked like there was a very large bulge in the front of those trunks. Bulldog couldn't help but think to himself that those were the ugliest undershorts he had ever seen in his life. He wondered if they were worth it, though, for all of the pleasure Sean was about to receive.

"Nice body, man. Lean and strong, just the way I like it!" Axel said.

"Yeah, I work out. Can't stand fatties. You guys though, ya'll are nice and big and beefy. I love me some bear meat! The bigger the better, and you guys are huge…all over."

Sean started to open Axel's belt. The grizzled biker wasn't wearing anything under his pants; like most of his club brothers, he liked to go commando under his blue jeans. He liked the freedom of it. He liked how his cock and balls felt against the vibration of the bike when he rode. And, mostly, he simply liked the feeling of his big meat swinging between his legs as he walked and how it looked outlined against his pants. Bulldog, on the other hand, was unable to go commando. He had to wear a jockstrap under his pants to hold his massive member in check. If he didn't, he would never be able to ride his bike or do much else. As Axel pushed his jeans down his legs, his rock-hard nine inches of uncut biker cock jutted out from his hairy groin. Sean's face lit up like a kid who just got the Christmas present he'd been waiting for all year.

"What are you waiting for, Sean? You wanted this, now go for it! Knock yourself out," Axel said. Sean didn't have to be told twice. He bent down and opened his mouth to take the massive knob of Axel's cock into his mouth. The feeling of the man's tongue on his cockhead was incredible and Axel's hands went to the back of Sean's head and gripped it lightly. Sean started to lick the swollen helmet as his hand wrapped around the base and held it steady, feeling the throbbing of the big man's heartbeat.

Bulldog was watching with desire and wasn't going to be left out. He could feel his own meat swelling with anticipation. He pushed his jeans down his legs and over his big boots. His massive organ was already starting to rise to its full size. Bulldog moved his right hand down to Sean's asshole and fingered the outside of it lightly. It was tight. He thought to himself that it wouldn't be for much longer. Sean moved his hand back and gripped Bulldog's swelling organ. He could not believe what he was holding in his hand. He took Axel's cock out of his mouth and turned his head to look. He stared in wonder at the mammoth endowment of the biker behind him. Bulldog's mighty prick was now fully hard and swollen to its full 12-inch length and beer bottle thickness. The big, hung biker knew that there was no way in hell his cock was going to get into that hole without some assistance and some lube, so he started to probe Sean's hole with his thick digits.

For Sean, the feeling of Bulldog's fingers slipping into his hole was pure pleasure. He might have called out had he not had his mouth stuffed once more with the thick, arched cock of Axel. Sean was having a hard time accommodating the banana-curved man-stick of Axel, but he wasn't going to give up – it felt too good. He could feel the deep probing of Bulldog's fingers and groaned with excitement with each exploratory poke the big man made to his behind. He could feel himself starting to get hard and wet and that made it even easier for Bulldog to explore.

"MMMMMM….Mmmmm…..Uuuhhhhhh," Sean moaned as he slobbered Axel' big cock.

"Damn, this boy is a good cocksucker! Maybe we should keep him around as a bitch after this is all over," Axel suggested. Bulldog knew that wouldn't be the case. Guests of the party were never kept around afterward. The bitches were a special consideration and were collected in other ways. Guests never stayed longer than one party – strict club rules.

"Let's just get this done with. I'm horny as hell!" Bulldog said, as he turned and lined up his cock with the tight hole of the man. Sean felt the head of the biker's monster-sized meat against the opening of his rectum and tried to pull his mouth off of Axel's to tell Bulldog that he wanted him badly and he couldn't wait. He had also came to the realization that this was the biggest cock he had even been about to take and the thought excited him so much that his own cock was twitching with anticipation. He never got the chance to say a word – suddenly Axel grabbed the boy's head and brought his gaze back onto Axel's member. Sean started to smile and went back to work lapping his tongue around Axel's tip, slowly drawing the precum out and then taking it all in.

"Don't worry, Sean, I ain't gonna fuck you dry… I'll get it nice and wet for you!" Bulldog said as he spat into his hand and coated the end of his cock with the saliva. He then spat on Sean's hole and pressed the end of his cock against the opening again. Sean braced himself. He knew there was nothing that could stop the pleasure he was about to experience and he couldn't wait. He knew when he hooked up with guys like this, that it was always a gamble. These were real men, hard men and tough men. Men like these were sometimes great, sometimes terrible when they wanted some from a fuck toy. Now, looking back at Bulldog, he knew he struck the jackpot with this pair. He knew he was in for a good time.

"Here it comes, man!" Bulldog said as he started to press his cockhead into the boy's delicate starfish.

"Yeah brother! Plow it in there. Tear him up good!" Axel had started to give a full-on face fuck to Sean, who was now lapping it up with every stroke in of the biker's thick prong. Bulldog knew that the boy's hole was ready to give up its treasures but he was not ready for the level of stick sweet wetness he was met with. He pressed his boots to the floor and gave a solid shove forward with his hips. His egg-sized knob forced its way inside of Sean who let out a loud shout of pleasure, which, even muffled by the giant cock buried in his throat was clearly audible. Bulldog took it as his sign to keep going. He continued to press inch after inch of his pole into Sean's backside. He knew he was more than Sean had ever taken before but he also knew that Sean was more than ready to take it all in. At this point, the trio was already started on a course they were powerless to alter, so they though they might as well make it a hell of a ride and let them all enjoy it.

"Yeah, big man! Skewer him good! Make him all yours!" said Axel excitedly as he continued to mouth-fuck Sean, slamming his cock in and out of the boy's mouth with an aggressive, almost violent stroke. Bulldog was now fully buried in the boy's ass to his balls and was flexing his cock inside Sean's rectum to give the boy a little thrill. He knew he was putting great pressure on the young man's prostate and that it must feel incredible for Sean. He held this position for a few moments to give Sean's body a chance to grow accustomed to the size and hardness of the mass of man meat inside of him. Sean moaned with delight, telling Bulldog how good it felt to have the biker inside him.

Sean had never had anything that big inside of him in his life. He could not believe that the big biker had managed to get that giant thing into him so easily. What he didn't know was how good it would feel. It felt better than anything he had felt before. Bulldog pulled back about halfway and waited a moment before he pushed forward again. Once more the boy screamed out with pleasure around Axel's cock.

"Keep doing that, brother! Every time he moans like that it makes his throat vibrate around my stiffy. Feels amazing," Axel said.

Bulldog could not believe how crude these men he called brothers could be at times. Of course he had also seen the other side of them on many occasions. It was the balance that made them family. Just as with any family, there were things he did not agree with, but he accepted them and made the best of it. Soon, Bulldog was fucking Sean's hole with a faster pace, a full-stroking fervor that was pleasurable to him and to Sean taking in his entire long, thick spear.

"Yeah...that's it, boy! Keep working that cock! DAMN!" said Axel as he pounded his prick in and out of Sean's mouth with powerful strokes. He intermittently pushed his cock all the way into Sean's throat and held it there, grinding his powerful hips to make the boy take it even deeper once more. He was amazed that Sean was taking it all in and actually asking for more "Fuck yeah!"

Bulldog knew he needed to hurry up his fuck. He had incredible self-control and, if he wanted to, he would be able to fuck Sean's wet hole all night long. But he knew there wasn't that much time. The moon was almost at its apex and when it reached that point it would be time for the main event of the evening – the feast – and then, after that, the all-important running of the pack. He started to concentrate on what he was doing. He could feel it building inside him. He could see that Axel was reaching his point of no return as well.

Sean moaned as he felt Bulldog's pace increasing and his strokes growing even more powerful. He knew the big man was about to cum. The realization suddenly hit him that the biker was not wearing any protection, but he knew that despite the risky lifestyle of the outlaw, there was nothing he could do about it now. He was stuck between them, impaled on both ends by their big cocks. He was going to get both their loads – one in his mouth and one up his ass – and he couldn't wait. He had a good feeling that these were not the kind of men who pulled out and he was right. Outside Bulldog could hear sounds of more fucking going on around the camp. The bikers were making use of the guests and the guests sounded like they were all enjoying themselves.

"Getting close, brother!" Axel exclaimed.

"Me too, man!" Bulldog answered.

"Then let's do this!" Axel pushed deep one last time and then pulled his cock out of the man's mouth and tilted Sean's head back. He aimed his knob at Sean's tongue and let loose a stream of thick white cream that streaked across Sean's face and then started to pool in the back of the boy's throat. As he released his load, he threw his head back and started to growl. His body tensed up and, as he looked back down at Sean, he made a seething sound through his teeth. Bulldog looked at his biker brother. His eyes were glowing as the power of his orgasm threatened to trigger a change. That was one of the hardest things to deal with as a wolf – any powerful emotion could trigger a change that was potentially uncontrollable.

Sean could not see what was happening to Axel. What he did know was that he couldn't believe how much cum came out of the biker's cock. There was more sticky sweet cum in his mouth than he had ever seen come out of a man's cock in all his life. It was thick and creamy, almost like mayonnaise. He gulped but it was hard to swallow. It coated the back of his throat and his esophagus as it slid down. The taste was rich and bitter, better than any man juice he had tasted before. It was salty but also sweet, thanks to the enormous amount of beer that the thuggish brute drank on a daily basis.

On the other end, Sean could feel Bulldog also releasing his load. Bulldog was fighting the urge to let his wolf come out. He was gripping Sean's hips hard with his hands, his fingernails growing longer with the potential of his transformation, lightly digging into the man's skin. He started to convulse as he pumped rope after rope of his own thick, creamy cum into the man. He growled as he pumped his load out and held his position, his cum pouring out and filling Sean's tingling insides.

He pulled his cock out of Sean's hole and a backwash of cum came with it. It ran down Sean's legs as Bulldog pulled up his pants and turned to walk out the door of the shed. "I didn't tell you to stop, did I? Keep sucking till you're told not to! I have a bit more for you…" Axel growled.

As Bulldog opened the door of the shed, he found one of his biker brothers standing outside. As he left the shed the other biker pushed his way in and unfastened his pants to haul out his own rock-hard cock. Bulldog watched as he slipped into Sean's well-opened hole easily, using Bulldog's cum as his lube. Bulldog walked around to the front of the cabin and looked around. Sure enough, the party was in full swing. There were sexual couplings of two, three or more bikers and a "guest" in every direction. He looked up at the deck and saw the "servants" eagerly looking at the moon and getting more and more anxious with every passing second.

The club "servants" were two gay boys and two straight girls who took care of the needs of the club and tended to its members. They were all gathered on the porch. They saw that things were getting close to culmination and started to make their way inside. They knew what was coming and knew that the safest place for them to be was in the cubbyhole under the floor in the front room. They had been through this enough times to know that once the feast started the men were not too discerning about who and what they ate. These four total humans had proven themselves loyal to the club for various reasons. They were taken care of, protected, provided for and, most of all, allowed to live in exchange for their loyalty and service. They were, for all intents and purposes, the club's property and the men never ceased to make good use of their services in every way possible.

Bulldog could tell that the main event was almost upon them as well. He buttoned up his pants and started to walk away from the shed. As he got a couple of yards away he heard Sean say to the other biker: "Ouch! Careful with the fingernails, big man..." Bulldog knew then that it was starting.

Bulldog did what he always did on moon nights. He walked down to the lakeshore and sat on the large boulder by the water. He looked out at the lake where the mirror surface of the water reflected the bright moonlight. In the distance, he heard the first growls followed by screams. The screaming didn't last long. Wolves liked to go for the throat first; that brought an end to the screaming quickly enough. There were only five "guests" at the party that night and 14 bikers were there. He knew it would not take long with those types of numbers. He closed his eyes and started in his mind to sing the lullaby that his mom used to sing for him when he was a child. He blocked out the sounds of the "feast" going on up the hill. He preferred to think of the peace of the woods and the beauty of nature that surrounded him.

It was only half an hour until the screaming, the growling and the howling came to a stop. He waited another couple of minutes before he turned and walked back to the camp. When he got there, he found his fellow bikers and pack brothers standing around the campsite covered in blood and in various states of undress. Some were still gnawing at pieces of flesh while others were busy taking off what remained of their clothing. There was a mix of emotions running though Bulldog as he walked into the scene, just as there was every month when he returned to the camp after the "feast." Part of him was attracted to the sight of the carnage and the smell of fresh blood, but part of him was put off by the fact that only a short while ago those innocent young men had no idea of the fate that was in store for them.

"My brothers. We have partied and we have feasted," declared Charlie, the biker leader and alpha male of the pack as he stepped to the top step of the deck and looked out among his brothers. "We have indulged our carnal desires for sex and we have satisfied our natural hunger for meat and blood. Now let us worship the moon as our people have for generations. Let us go forth and experience the freedom that only we know is possible, as our ancestors did before us. We own the night. We are the rulers of it. We are the kings of nature and these woods are our Kingdom!"

The rest of the men started to howl and hoot at the words. There was a sense of pride in Bulldog as well, but he was more subdued about it. The rest of the bikers began to strip off their clothes and left these lying in piles around the camp. The humans would come out and collect it all and put it in neat piles while the pack was out running. Bulldog started to strip off his own clothes as well, leaving them in a pile at his feet. Soon all of the bikers were naked and gathered near the bonfire.

"It's gonna be a good run, brother!" Mason, another biker, said as he twisted his neck side-to-side and then started to roll his shoulders to loosen them up. He still had blood all over his face from his part in the feast.

"Yes it is – a good night for a run and a damn good meal!" Vince said as he let out a belch and patted his stomach. "That little

Chinese girl was tasty, but then again, I've always loved Asian food!" He emitted an obnoxious laugh that was shared by several of the men around them. Bulldog was sickened by the comment.

"What's wrong, brother? See, this is what happens when you don't take fresh meat and blood on moon nights: you start to get crabby all the time!" Vince chided Bulldog.

"Let's just run and save the conversations, okay Vince?" Bulldog said.

"Suits me fine! Everything you say bores the hell out of me anyway!" Vince stepped away to move closer to the front of the pack.

"Brothers, let's run!" Charlie shouted as he closed his eyes and leapt forward, changing into his wolf form as he flew through the air. The rest of the bikers began to change and run after their leader. Bulldog concentrated on the fire burning within his soul and lurched forward as his body morphed into his animal form. He suddenly felt the cool, hard ground beneath his paws and sped off after his brothers.

*****

The next morning after the party, Bulldog woke up and looked around. He was in the back bedroom of the cabin and one of the bitches was between his legs slowly sucking his massive cock. His morning wood was calling out for a release but it had nothing to do with the product of his big balls; instead he needed to drain his bladder of all of the beer he had consumed the night before. He gently pushed the boy away from his cock and dragged himself to his feet.

"Not right now, Al." He stepped away from the boy. The other two humans were cuddled up with each other in the corner of the room. On moon nights they liked to sleep with Bulldog in the back room just to be on the safe side. They knew he didn't eat and that he would keep them safe from the others in case they started to get out of hand. He made his way to the bathroom and pissed before stepping into the main room and locating his clothes. The others liked to run around naked all the time but that wasn't for him.

He tried to ignore the carnage that was still present all around the camp. He walked up to the deck and found a few leftover meatballs and a nearly solid clump of cheese dip that would have to be his breakfast. When he had finished the food, along with a chunk of toast, he walked toward his bike. A black and white checkerboard shoe was lying on the ground near his Harley. It was streaked with blood. Those were the shoes that Sean had been wearing. He shook his head and got on his bike. He pulled out of the camp and made his way toward town. He would let his brothers clean up the mess that was left behind. He hadn't eaten and didn't think he should have to dispose of the leftovers.

Bulldog drove into town and parked his bike on Main Street. Then he went into Jazzy Java Joe's Coffee House and walked up to the counter. He ordered the same thing that he ordered every morning: a Grande double brew French roast, black, with a shot of espresso. The boy behind the counter was new and, apparently, was also an idiot, as Bulldog had to tell him the order three times before he understood what it was he wanted.

While he was waiting for his drink to be made, Bulldog looked around at what was going on in the coffee shop. It was the same old thing had seen in the place a hundred times. It seemed that Joe's never changed. It was still the same place it had been when he had first walked into it seven years ago. From what he had been told, it was the same as it had been when it opened more than five years before that. There was a certain comfort in things that never changed, but at the same time there was also an excitement in the new. And there was one new thing that suddenly caught Bulldog's eye in the coffee shop.

Standing at the end of the counter was a husky man with a perfectly shaved head: the new manager. He wore a mint green shirt and a pair of front-pleated khaki trousers. He had a salt-and-pepper goatee and mustache and looked like he made use of a tanning bed and the local gym. He was what many would refer to as a bear. Bulldog found himself admiring the man and even got caught looking at him on a couple of occasions. The bear was going over some figures on a clipboard and occasionally taking sips out of a 20 ounce bottle that was sitting on the counter. The thing that Bulldog found most interesting was the fact that every now and then, every few moments, the man would turn and steal a look at him. He wasn't sure why the man kept staring at him. Maybe he was trying to figure out if Bulldog was trouble, or maybe he was just curious about the customers and Bulldog had caught his attention for some reason.

Bulldog stood at the counter and waited for his order to be served. Joe's place was not the best coffee house but it was the only one in town. Besides, they had good desserts and the prices were fair. The thing that Bulldog liked the most was that it was the kind of place where you could sit quietly and read, or check e-mails or just close your eyes and decompress without anyone being too judgmental. It was a laid-back place. Bulldog liked places like this: places that allowed people to just be themselves without having to make excuses for it.

As Bulldog waited, another customer was being served. He was asking for a lot of pastries to be packed to go. The boy behind the counter seemed to be more interested in taking care of that task than in helping to fill the order he had taken from Bulldog. It was very annoying. The boy needed to learn how to handle one task at a time, Bulldog thought.

The boy finally made the order and then sat Bulldog's order on the upper part of the counter, turning to collect the next order for the other customer. As he turned back around to hand the pastries to the other man, his arm swept the top of the counter and knocked over the coffee that Bulldog was putting sweetener and creamer into. The cup went flying off the counter and the hot coffee landed all over Bulldog, saturating his black T-shirt and his leather club vest. Immediately, Bulldog was furious.

"What the fuck, asshole?" he said, trying to keep his calm.

"Sorry, man. My bad." The barista all but ignored the consequences of what he had just done and the significance of it.

"'My bad?' That's all you can say? 'My bad'…? What the hell are you doing? You ruined my jacket." Bulldog demanded.

"Hey, like I said, sorry, man. Geez. It's no big deal," replied the barista.

"It's a very big deal. You need to be more careful – you don't know who you're messing with!"

"Hey, it's not like it's gonna make a difference. Looks like your clothes could use a good run through the washer anyway," the boy replied arrogantly. Bulldog reached over and grabbed the boy by the upper arm and pulled him halfway across the counter. "Hey, let me go!" the boy exclaimed.

"Look here, you little shit. I don't know who the hell you think you are talking to, but I am not the man you want to fuck with."

"Excuse me! Is there some problem here?" The man with the shaved head stepped over to where the altercation was taking place. Bulldog let go of the boy's arm and the barista stepped away from the counter.

Bulldog gave the barista a sneer and went to sit down and clean himself off.

"Look, I'm really sorry about that," said the manager as he walked over to where Bulldog was sitting. The big biker was still fuming over the encounter but was trying to remain composed. He knew that if he let himself get angry, there would be bigger problems than just spilled coffee and a punk with a bad attitude.

"It's no big deal," Bulldog said.

"Well, it's a big deal to me. I'm the manager and I want to make sure all of my customers are happy. I would appreciate it if you would let me pick up the bill for dry cleaning your vest, and also, next time you come in, please let me know and whatever you want is on the house. Hell, I tell you what, call it in, you and your buddies, and I will deliver it to your clubhouse or whatever." Steve said. Bulldog looked up at him with a quizzical look on his face.

"Why would you want to do that?" he asked.

"Because, well, I don't judge people, and I don't think that someone should be mistreated because of how they dress or how they live their life. There is too much of that going on in the world."

Suddenly it made sense. The white sedan in the parking lot with the rainbow gay bear paw bumper sticker must belong to this guy. Bulldog looked him over carefully. He would have never known it by looking at him. Steve, as his nametag said, looked like just any other middle management, shirt-and-tie nerd. Bulldog had to admit, though, that he did think the guy was kind of cute, if a bit naïve.

"Yeah, I guess there is. So that's your Mercury in the lot?" Bulldog asked. Steve smiled and looked to the side for a second.

"Yes…is it that obvious?" Steve asked.

"Not at all. In fact, I'm a little shocked. I just put two and two together after what you just said, not to mention the fact that I did kind of notice you checking me out earlier." The biker took a sip from his coffee, smiling coyly.

"Sorry if I offended you. Not my intention."

"If I were offended, you would know. Make no mistake about that. Let's just say I have a bear paw myself, but it ain't no bumper sticker. Mine don't peel off." The man was shocked. Bulldog continued: "Let me guess, I don't look the type?"

"Well…no. Not at all," Steve replied. "Well…it's nice to meet you…" The man extended his hand.

"People call me Bulldog…" the biker replied, accepting the handshake.

"It's nice to meet you, Bulldog. My name is Steve. I really do hope that I see you in here more often in the future." Steve smiled and then stepped away and returned behind the counter. He said something very stern to the barista that Bulldog could not make out, but the intent was obvious as the boy yanked off his apron, grabbed his keys and phone from under the counter and started to storm out.

"This place sucks anyway! We need a real coffee house in this town, like Starbucks! Oh and everyone: the cheesecake is pre-made and frozen!" the boy screamed as he left the building.

Bulldog was still shocked. He most certainly had not expected that. He had never had someone stand up for him in this way before. He had gotten used to the idea of being abused and stereotyped because of the clothes he wore, the machine he rode, the life he lived and the guys he ran with. When he put that patch on, he knew he was entering a life that would put him on the edge of society and he was okay with that. He didn't like society. It asked too many questions and made too many demands. The club, the pack, offered him the chance to be whom and what he was without all the drama of the "normal" world. He looked over to where Steve was standing and smiled at him. He got up and walked to the counter and whispered to Steve: "I like the cheesecake. See you tomorrow." He walked out of the coffee shop.

Once Bulldog was in the parking lot, he looked back at the shop. There was something about the guy that made him look forward to his coffee the next morning. He straddled his bike and started it up. Steve looked out the window. He too was looking forward to the next time they met. He only hoped it would lead to something more.

*****

# Volume Two - Nomad

It was morning. Bulldog was up early, and felt surprisingly excited about the day, despite the fact that it was a very ugly morning with rain falling steadily outside and the threat of a thunderstorm in the area. He opened his eyes and felt…happy. He had not been so chipper on waking in a long time. He had even jumped in the shower and put on a clean pair of blue jeans and a fresh t-shirt. He put on his chaps and heavy jacket against the rain. They wouldn't prevent him from being soaked to the skin by the time that he got to where he was going, but it would help. He waited around for a little while for at least a lessoning in the rain and then jumped on his bike and headed out. He was lucky, it wasn't that far of a ride to where he was heading, but as was the standard with Bulldog and his luck about two blocks from his destination the clouds opened up and the threatening thunderstorm came to bear. Bulldog gritted his teeth and dealt with it, even that could not break the good mood that he was in.

He came to a stop at the red light of the intersection that had Joe's on the corner. He looked over at the parking lot and was actually giddy when he saw that the white car with the striped bear paw bumper sticker was in the same spot that it had been the day before. He pulled through the intersection and into the lot. He parked the bike in a spot where he would be able to see it though the large side window of the coffee house despite the fact that there were plenty of better spots much closer to the door. He loved his bike as most bikers did and he didn't like not being able to see it. As he walked into the front door of the place he knew why there were so many prime parking spots available. He had never in all of years of coming to Joe's seen it as empty as it was right then. The place was all but abandoned with the exception of an older man wearing khakis and a cardigan sweater eating a breakfast sandwich and drinking a large latte while reading the morning paper. Bulldog looked around, and then walked toward the counter where a pretty young girl was standing. He had never seen her before and assumed that she was the replacement for the inept idiot that had been fired the day before. The only other person that he saw was the older woman who had worked at the place for years. He could never remember her name but she was polite enough. Honestly it had surprised Bulldog that they had brought in a new manger from outside, he would have thought that if anyone was going to replace Jimmy when he left it would have been her. He imagined that the owner had a good reason for not making that choice though and he had to admit that he was glad that he had. If he had promoted the old woman then he would not have ever met Steve.

The door to the kitchen swung open and Steve came walking out to the front service area with his iPad in his hand. He looked up to see Bulldog walking toward the counter and he suddenly found himself smiling. "Suzie, why don't you go and work on those materials that I gave you. I can handle the "rush…" If you have any question just let me know," he said as he took over at the cash register.

"Well, I'm not sure you will be able to handle this all by yourself Steve," Bulldog said as he smiled at the manager with an innocent schoolboy look on his face.

"Yeah, it's the weather. Normally when we have rain it actually drives business in. When it comes to a thunderstorm though, everybody wants to just stay in till the danger has passed which I guess I can more than understand," Steve said. "Speaking of which; you look like a drowned rat."

"Well, yeah, but I didn't want to take a chance..." Bulldog said. Suddenly realizing that he had let slip out a little too much information.

"On what?" Steve asked.

"On…well not getting my coffee. I didn't want to take a chance on not getting my coffee," Bulldog replied. He hoped that he had covered the slip well enough, but he could tell that he hadn't and felt self-conscious.

"Well, since you did battle the elements and made it all the way here, what can I get for you, big man?" Steve asked.

"I'll just take…" Bulldog said as he looked up at the menu board as if he was reading it, "Hell, who am I kidding? I'll just take the same thing I take every morning. Grande double brew French roast, black, with a shot of espresso, and a croissant. Also, this morning I think I will treat myself a little and have one of those blueberry scones that look so good in the case there." Steve smiled and rung up the order before cancelling it out with his mangers ID.

"I tell you what. Why don't you head over there and have a seat I will bring it over in just a few minutes," Steve said. Bulldog was shocked that he had not been asked to pay but he wasn't going to complain about the guy's generosity. He walked over to the table that he always sat at, the one in the corner between the fireplace and the big picture window that looked out to where his bike was parked and took a seat. He normally stared out the window and thought about what life outside of the town and outside of the club would be like. This day though he found himself looking at the cute bear behind the counter and thinking more about the fact that he was one of the best looking guys and had the best personality of anyone he had met in a long time.

After several minutes Steve came over with a tray that had two cups of coffee and two small plates on it. One of the plates had the scone and not one but two croissants on it along with butter and honey, the other plate had a pecan pie filled donut, a specialty of the house and another croissant. He sat the tray down on the table, "mid if I join you, I haven't had breakfast yet myself."

"Not at all, please, I would enjoy the company." Bulldog said.

"Would you like me to turn the fire on? Might help you to dry out a little faster." Steve asked.

"Nah, that's okay. No point. I'm just sure to get wet again today. Hell, from the looks of things, more than once today," Bulldog replied.

"True. I know it's a pain in the ass for guys like you, but I love the rain. I find it to be refreshing, thought provoking, even romantic," Steve said. Bulldog looked over at him over the edge of his coffee cup. Steve started to blush as he realized the way that must have come out.

"I love the rain. Where I'm originally from in Montana it either rains or snows a little almost every afternoon depending on the season. Love the rain, but hate being on the bike in it. Thinking one of these days I may break down and buy a truck for bad weather, but then there would be a lot of flak from the guys over that," Bulldog stated.

"Yeah, that whole biker thing does tend to lend itself to being on the bike I suppose," Steve said as he spread some butter on his croissant.

"Yep…"

"So have you always been a biker? I mean, is it a family thing like it is with some guys, born into it?" Steve asked.

"No not at all, I was actually born the son of a university professor. He worked at the college in the Montana town that I grew up in." Bulldog said.

"That explains that." Steve said.

"In what way?"

"Your mannerisms, your method of speaking, the words that you use. They indicate that you are very educated and come from the cultured background. Not necessarily what you would expect from a typical biker, at least not from what I know of your lifestyle, which I do admit is limited," Steve said.

"Yeah, he was a professor of archeology. Very refined man. He pushed me from an early age to do well in school and expand my mind. The problem was that I expanded it a little too much. Led to some serious disagreements between us, formed a wedge as I got older. That wedge is what eventually led to my walking out from him and leaving town. I have not been back since."

"Ain't family great? And your mother if I may ask?" Steve inquired.

"She left us at an early age. Couldn't handle the life of being the wife of an archeologist. When my dad wasn't teaching, which was an all-consuming passion for him, he was traipsing around the world to dig sites or on exploration expeditions. She left when I was 9 she stayed in touch for a couple of years but then she just dropped out of our lives. We would get cards or an occasional letter but never anything significant. She got caught up into her own career I suppose."

"And what did she do?" Steve asked.

"She was an anthropological Linguist. She studied dead languages and how they impacted modern development," Bulldog replied. "Enough about me, how the hell did you end up in this arm pit of a town?"

"Well, I was in a relationship for 12 years, thought everything was great and then one day I came home to find him in bed with another man."

"Ouch…that sucks. Was it someone that you knew?" Bulldog asked.

"You could say that. It was my best friend," Steve said casually. Bulldog almost choked on his coffee when he heard the statement.

"That's…different." Steve started to chuckle at the response.

"To say the least. Needless to say, that was the end of the marriage, and the end of my contact with my best friend. Well sort of. I went to his office and confronted him the day that I moved out of the house. I told him I had no idea that he was gay and asked him why he never said anything to me. He said that he didn't know until the very moment that he was cumming in Jerry's mouth the first time. From then on there was no doubt in his mind. Apparently this had been going on for a while. I'm not sure how it got started, didn't ask, didn't really even want to know. I left town that afternoon and as you said, never looked back."

"Well, at least it wasn't awkward," Bulldog said with a chuckle. Outside the storm was passing and people were beginning to filter into the coffee house.

"I guess you have to get to work now huh?" Bulldog said.

"Yeah, I guess I do. This was nice though. I hope that we can do it again soon," He said as he stood up and began to clear the debris from the table.

"How about tomorrow morning? Same time?" Bulldog asked with a smile on his face. He stood and began to get himself together as well.

"I would like that Bulldog…"

"BD. Just call me BD everyone does." The biker said.

"Well that is more convenient. Does open the door for a lot of other possible interpretations, though," Steve said playfully.

"Yes it does, and many of those may be well earned," Bulldog replied.

"Really? That sounds like a conversation for another day. Be careful out there, BD, things are going to be very slick for a few hours," Steve said as he turned and started to walk away. "See you tomorrow."

"Yes, you will," Bulldog said as he walked toward the door.

*****

Bulldog walked into the clubhouse of the Beasts M.C. and walked over to one of the tables. He sat down and looked over at the TV where the baseball game was being on. "Hell of a game. Want a beer?" Charlie said as he stepped over and pulled the other chair at the table back. He swung his leg over the back of the chair high and wide, as if he was mounting his Harley. It was a habit that all of them had. It was just a natural development of straddling a motorcycle every single day.

"Nah, maybe just a soda." Bulldog replied.

"You there. Bring the man a soda," Charlie said to one of the clubs female attendants. She quickly brought Bulldog a can of soda and a small glass with a couple of ice cubes.

"Thanks," he said as he took the bottle from her and opened it. Charlie looked at him quizzically as if he had done some horrible injustice to the world by saying thank you to a person who was for all effects and purposes a slave. "Glad I got to see you today. Wanted to talk to you, Bull."

"Well, here I am boss, talk away," Bulldog replied.

"I'm worried about you brother. We all are."

"Worried about what?" Bulldog asked as he took a long drink of the soda and focused his attention on the ballgame on TV.

"You are getting more and more distant. Every day it seems you are drifting further away from the club and its core, the brotherhood. Take last night for example, first you didn't take part in the feast..."

"I never do and you know it, you also know why. We have had this discussion to the point of it making me nauseous. You guys do whatever you want. I don't have to kill innocent people and eat their bodies to be a part of this pack, to be your brother. I do everything else that is asked of me and I am there for everything that this club gets into. Hell, most of the time I am on the front line ready to do whatever it takes for this club, for this pack. I will not take innocent blood though. I'm sorry. I just can't be a part of that," Bulldog said as he leaned back and put his big boots up onto the table crossing one foot over the other and once again looking at the TV.

"I understand that, Bull, but there are other things. The guys just think that you are getting too far away from the heart of the club. Is there anything that I can do to make you feel like you are a connected part of this pack again?"

"I just don't feel like myself anymore. I feel like there is something missing from my life. Something that I can't put a word on, something that is more than just all of this. Do you have any idea what I am talking about?"

"No, I can't say that I do. But then, you came to us from a world that was far different than this. I was born into this. Natural wolf and third generation biker. I guess, to a degree, I have always known that this day may come, when you started to wonder if you made the right choice all those years ago." Charlie said taking a drink form his beer and, realizing he had finished it, motioning to the same girl who had brought Bulldog his soda to bring him another.

"Don't get me wrong. I don't regret that choice. I joined up with you guys and it saved me. I love you guys but there is a fire inside of me that I just can't get sorted. I feel like there is more to life than just this and I want to find out what that is. If nothing more than just to know that I found it and put a name to it," Bulldog replied.

"Is there anything that I can do, that the club can do to help you with that brother?"

"Actually, there is one thing. I have been giving this a lot of thought. Let me go nomad for a year. Let me get out of this town, away for all of this and find what it is that I feel I am missing in my life. When I get back, I will more than likely be the Bulldog that I have always been," Bulldog said.

"Bull, you know that is not possible. No member of the club has gone Nomad in over 30 years. It's too dangerous. If you were out there on your own and something was to happen, or you were to get exposed as what you are, then it would come back on us and hurt us all," Charlie responded. It was not the answer that Bulldog wanted to hear. He had known however that it was the answer that he would most likely get and that this would be the end of the discussion on the subject.

"Well, I don't know of much else that may be of help. I guess you guys will have to just get used to me like this until I either figure it out or I eat a bullet," Charlie stood up and looked down at him.

"Brother, I can tell that you're hurting. I want to help. I can't offer that you think you need, but I beg you to find what it is that can help you within the boundaries of what is an option," He stepped away and left Bulldog to his own devices. Even as he sat there mulling the conversation he had just had with Charlie over in his mind, he had a smile, ever so slight as it was, come over his face, as he thought back to the nice conversation he had with Steve at the coffee house that morning. He looked forward to the next day when he could see him again. The smile got bigger.

*****

It had been two and half weeks that the men had been sharing their mornings together sitting at the same table by the fire, watching people come and go to and from the coffee house, watching traffic outside the big picture window, enjoying random conversation and just being happy to have the other in their lives for about an hour every morning. On Monday night Steve was just getting ready for bed after a day from hell where it seemed that every possible thing that could have went wrong at the coffee house did, and in some cases more than once. He was used to the idea of bad Mondays. He didn't know of anything that could mean a good Monday in his book, but this Monday was one for the annals of history. He was stripped down to his underwear following a much-needed long hot shower, and was just crawling into bed when the thought of Bulldog came into his mind. He started to smile as he pulled the covers over himself and grabbed the remote to switch on the TV. Leno was on and he loved to watch the funny newspaper headlines segment.

As he watched the TV, flipping to a basketball game, he found his mind kept returning to Bulldog. He thought about his large body, his ragged salt and pepper goatee, and his sparkling steel grey eyes. He thought about the deep laugh that he let out when he found something funny, he thought about the heavy sinew covered arms, covered with tattoos and strong from the daily effort put into the controlling of his motorcycle. He thought about the man's smell, the combination of his own natural scent, which Steve found intoxicating, and the crisp fresh scent of the ivory soap that he showered with. It was that which got his mind floating to places that were of the more exotic. The smell of Bulldog. It was unlike anything that he had ever smelled before. He had a scent that was powerful yet subtle. He could not explain it, but he didn't have to even attempt to explain what that smell did to him.

As he thought about it and those grey eyes that he could just fall into and keep falling forever he started to feel the effect in the front of his underwear. He pushed the covers back and looked own at the rapidly growing tent that was forming in the pouch of his white cotton briefs. He moved his hand down to the heavy bulge that was becoming even more pronounced by the second. The heat, the heft of his manhood was incredible in his hand. He could already feel himself starting to throb as he grew stiff. He hooked his thumbs under the waistband of his briefs and pulled the front of them down to allow his thick hard cock to spring forth from its cotton prison.

He let his finger gently graze the now tightly stretched skin of his circumcised cock. The sensations were electric as his thumb began to trace the thick vein that ran along the top of his shaft from the base to the head. His forefinger touched the delicate spot under the head of his cock on the bottom side and he felt as if he was going to explode right then and there. He stopped for a moment and thought about how long it had been since he had allowed himself to indulge in a little personal fun. It had been far too long. He reached over and opened the drawer to the nightstand and took out the bottle of silicon-based lube that was there. He popped the cap and squirted a small amount of the liquid into the palm of his hand. He wrapped his hand around his swollen throbbing cock and started to gently slid his fist up and down as he closed his eyes and let his mind wander to another place and another time, a place and time that had not yet happened and for all he knew might not ever happen despite his intense desire for it to.

"You are so incredibly sexy," Steve said as he looked deep into Bulldog's eyes.

"I have waited for this for a long time. You sure you can handle me?" Bulldog said as he let his hands roam over the large hairy body of Steve.

"I don't care how big you are; I want you. I want your body, your heart, your mind, your soul. I want you, big man, and I want you now," Steve said.

His hand was now moving up and down his thick shaft with a purpose. In his mind he was slowly lowering himself down to his knees. The big biker brute now towering over him, looking down at him like a domineering god clad in leather and denim. He had never been the kind to go for the bad boy type but there was something about Bulldog that was different. He reached up and started to unfasten Bulldog's belt and open the button on the fly of his grimy jeans. As he pulled the fly open he was greeted with the sight of the outlaws' large uncut cock hanging free and flaccid in his pants unencumbered by any type of underwear. He moved his hand up to take ahold of the incredible piece of manhood that hung between the big man's large hairy thighs, slowly pulling the foreskin back to reveal the shiny reddish purple head underneath.

Steve's hand was now moving faster and faster up and down his own thick shaft as he thought about the feeling of the oversized meat of Bulldog in his hand. He was getting close but he wanted this fantasy to last so he slowed his pace. He moved his mouth close to the slowly stiffening cock of Bulldog and let his lips lightly graze the top of his shaft. The big man's long pole was quickly starting to rise to its impressive size. He lifted the end of it and moved it toward his mouth. He had to maintain control to keep from cumming as he moved his hand up and down his own cock, his actions aided by the slick silicone lube. His lips moved close to the cock head of Bulldog who rested his hand on the shoulders of Steve and moved him ever closer to his meat pole with gentle pressure. His lips opened, he was only moments from taking the cock head in his mouth.

The loud ringing of his cellphone brought him back to reality and broke his concentration at the same time. A fire hose stream of thick white cum erupted from his cock, four long ropes streaked across his chest and clung to the thick forest of hair that was there. He threw his head back and slammed his free hand into the bed. He let go of his still dripping cock and grabbed his phone off the nightstand. He pressed the talk button, "Who are you and what do you want? I swear to god this better be good. What? WHAT! I don't care. Figure it out. Jesus Christ, didn't the previous manager, in all of the years that he was there, teach you people to do anything? It's not hard. Just press the reset button and the damn thing will turn off and turn itself back on after it cools down. Yes, I'm sure. Fine. Yes, I will talk to you tomorrow," he said as he hung up the phone and let out an exasperated grunt. He looked down at the mess that he had made on his chest and belly. He got up and went to the bathroom, using his underwear to clean up the slimy load and tossing them into the hamper. He put on a fresh pair, turned out the light, and went to sleep before anything else could go wrong.

*****

"Fucking Bitch!" Steve said as he hung up the phone and stuffed his cell back into his pocket. Bulldog was coming out of the pharmacy when he heard the sound and recognized his friend's voice. He looked in the direction of the exclamation and sure enough saw Steve standing beside his car looking distraught. He walked over wondering what in the world could make the normally cheerful and easy going bear get out of sorts to such a degree.

"Hey, Steve. Is everything okay?" Bulldog asked as he stuck out his hand to his friend.

"No, its not, but God am I glad to see you. At least you're a person I actually know who might be able to help me since that bitch on the phone was useless!" Steve said.

"Okay, well, why don't we start with what exactly she was being useless about and then see if we can figure it out from there," Bulldog said. At the same time the words were coming out of his mouth he looked over and saw the problem for himself. Steve's keys were still hanging in the ignition of the car and the doors were locked tight. "Ahh. I see now."

"Yeah and the fucking woman at the auto services company says she can't get a signal to the car to do a remote unlock. I don't remember my door pin number and she won't tell it to me either, she said she could reset it for me, but that would require being able to get a signal which would mean she…"

"Could just remotely unlock them. Yeah. Okay. Well, the good news is you're not totally screwed. I know a trick I can use to get the door open but you have to promise me that you won't ask questions. Just chalk it up to 'outlaw biker knowledge.' The bad news is that if I get the door open, you are gonna owe me a huge favor. Anything I want, anytime. One favor. Think you can handle that?" Bulldog said as Steve looked at him with a curious look. "I promise the favor won't be anything illegal or dangerous. You have my word."

"OK...sure I can go along with this. If nothing else, you have my interested piqued at this point. Hell, if you can get my car open I will do just about anything you could ask. I do not want to have to pay 150 bucks to a lock smith for something so stupid," Steve said. Bulldog smiled and turned toward the car door. He lifted the door handle and pressed a series of digits into the control panel. It was a much longer sequence than a normal keyless entry pin but after more than dozen key presses the door lock suddenly popped open.

"There you go!" Bulldog said stepping back with a *voila* flourish to his hand.

"How did you...?"

"All of these models have an emergency access bypass code for things like small children, elderly people, and pets who might be locked in the car. It's not common knowledge, of course, but I have a guy who taught it to me who used to work in a dealership," Steve put his arms around Bulldog and hugged him tight.

"Thank you so much," he said and then, realizing that the sexuality of the big biker brute might not be something that would be good to have public knowledge, backed off quickly and "butched" up his behavior. Bulldog smiled in gratitude for that.

"No problem. Now, as for that favor that you owe me, I think I'm going to cash in right now. What say you and I go out to grab a bite to eat one day soon, away from the coffee house?"

"Sure, I would like that. We can go grab a bite at Burger Hut or Shoney's, they have that lunch buffet. I guess you're a big eater huh," Bulldog got a look on his face of disappointment. Suddenly like a lightning bolt, it hit Steve what he had missed. "Wait, were you asking me out on a date, BD?"

"You know what, just forget it. I was stupid to even ask. I have to go. I'm glad you got the car open, was happy I could help. See you at the coffee house tomorrow?" Bulldog said.

"Now you just wait one minute! You can't just ask a person out on a date and then get all embarrassed and walk off without even hearing their answer. I know you're a biker but there is no need to be rude," Steve said with a wink.

"Uhhh, I'm a biker. Rude is kind of what I do."

"I'm not done talking, you didn't let me finish. I would love to go out on a date with you. I just wasn't sure that was what was going on, you know, with you being….well, what you are and this town being what it is, I wasn't sure that you were asking me another man to go out but if that was the case then yes, I would love to. Hell, I have been fighting the urge to ask you out since the first minute I realized we…were alike," Steve said. The sudden burst of assertiveness over the situation actually put Bulldog at ease.

"Okay then, if that's how you feel. Then yes, I would love to go out on a date with you and I have gotten to the point that I don't give a damn what the people of this Podunk town think about me or my lifestyle. I am sick and tired of being what everyone else wants me to be. So yes, Steve, I am asking you to go out with me tomorrow night for dinner and who the hell knows what else! We might actually go out for a movie too and see how scandalous we can get in the eyes of this back water shit hole of a town!" Bulldog said with a grin.

"Good! Then I accept. And you can pick me up at my house at 7! 1245 Hunser Road."

"Okay, I'll be there!" Bulldog said as he walked off and got onto his bike and rode away. Steve suddenly realized that was without a doubt the weirdest asking for date that probably had ever occurred and then started to laugh. He got into this car and started to pull out of the parking space when he realized he had still not gotten into the pharmacy to pick up his order. He laughed out loud again and got out of the car, this time making sure he had his keys in his hand.

*****

Bulldog pulled his Harley to a stop in front of Steve's house promptly at five minutes before seven. He didn't want to appear to be too early but at the same time he didn't want to waste a single minute that he had the chance to spend with Steve. He got off his bike and walked to the front door. After ringing the bell, he felt like a kid waiting for Christmas as he waited for Steve to answer the door. It took a couple of minutes and at first Bulldog started to wonder if he was being cast off. Suddenly the door opened and Steve was standing there in a pressed white shirt, with the collar open, and a pair of khakis. He looked even better than he did normally at work, even though he was dressed almost the same as he would have been at the coffee house. Bulldog was dressed in a hunter green microfiber shirt with a beige tie with small diamonds on it and a pair of brown khakis with hiking boots and black socks underneath. He had even put on a sexier pair of underwear and a white crew neck t-shirt. He felt like a history professor. Truth be told, he felt more like a dork.

"Wow, you look….great!" Bulldog said as he looked at his companion for the evening.

"And you look very different. I like it. You clean up nice, big man." Steve said.

"Thanks, I feel weird. It's been a long time since I had clothes like these on. Anyway. Shall we get going?" Bulldog said.

"I think we should." Steve responded. "Oh, by the way, I have a question, kind of personal, I hope you don't mind." Steve asked.

"Shoot."

"Well, just for tonight, considering that we are out on a nice date and we are both dressed the way we are, I was wondering if it was okay if I asked your real name? You don't have to tell me if you…"

"Lucas." Bulldog said. For some strange reason he felt 100% comfortable telling that to Steve, but he could not explain why.

"Lucas, huh? Wow, really, that's kind of cool. I never met a biker named Lucas before." Steve replied

"Well then, Steve, shall we head out? I have reservations at Café Roma for 8 and it's a bit of a drive to McKinley."

"I would be honored, Lucas. I assume we're taking my car?" He said.

"Yeah, might be best. Unless you wanted to take the bike," Bulldog replied.

"Whatever's best for you. But if we take my car, I have to stop and get gas. Café Roma. I have heard good things about that place," Steve said as they walked down the walk to the driveway and got into the car.

*****

The night started well but ended up with them having taco salads at the Taco Shack on Route 7. The trouble began when the waiter started to make fun of Bulldog for the way that he ordered the food and then for the selection of wine. Things then broke down even further with the manager eventually getting involved with the argument between the waiter and Bulldog. The biker got up and stormed out of the place without even paying the bill for the appetizers or the wine. After they ate at the Mexican cantina, they made their way back to Steve's house. Bulldog felt like a total failure, having not even been able to pull off being normal for one night out on the town with a great guy that he was crazy about.

"Well, this was a total disaster. I'm sorry that things went so bad. I should have known that this was a bad idea," Bulldog said.

"Hey! Hey you. NO! That's not your fault. Those people, they were just assholes. If they were not able to see the good guy in front of them then that is their fault. I don't care what others think, I am happy that you asked me out," Steve responded.

"Yeah, but it was so embarrassing for you to be in the middle of that," Bulldog said.

"Truth is, it didn't bother me one bit. But…if it's an issue for you then next time we will just have to have our date here and I will have to break down and fix a nice home cooked meal for you. I imagine it's been a while since you have had one," Steve said.

"I understand you don't want…wait, next time. You mean you want to see me again? Like this? I mean, like not just buddies at the coffee house?" Bulldog asked.

"Yes, Lucas Williams…" he made it a point to call him by his real name and not his biker name. The sound of it in Bulldog's ears was both foreign and somehow comforting at the same time. "I want to see you again. I like you. I want to get to know you and see, well I guess see where things go. If you are willing to deal with the drama from your club brothers then I can deal with the ridicule of this close-minded town. I have a feeling that you're worth it," Steve said as he leaned forward and kissed Bulldog lightly on the lips before stepping back and smiling as he opened the door.

"Uhhhh...Goodnight," Bulldog said as he smiled back.

"Goodnight," Steve replied and walked into the house closing the door behind him.

One thing that Steve said was true: there would be drama with the pack over this. So much drama, in fact, that Bulldog wasn't sure if he was fully prepared for it. But then again, he thought, that might not be a bad thing. "Things need to be shaken up a bit every now and then," he said as he stepped off the porch and walked to his bike. He felt like a long ride right then, with just him, the road and the moonlight. Things were going to be changing, and he hoped he was ready for it.

*****

# Volume Three – The Oath

Bulldog, Charlie, Axel, Damien, and Ray stood at the entrance to the driveway of the large split-story house on the outskirts of Birmingham. It was a nice neighborhood; most of the influential people of the city lived there. The very house that the men were standing in front of, accompanied by six of their biker brothers in full wolf form, was actually owned by a rental agency with a long-term lease being paid for by none other than state senator Gene Gillespie, representing the seventh district. Of course, the good representative did not live in the house himself. No, his home was in the state capital 90 miles away. The men had considered heading there instead, but thought better of it. They wanted to at least give Gillespie the chance to do right before they decided to tear his entire world apart. The house in question was currently occupied by a lovely young woman with whom the good legislator was found of keeping company, when he was not in the mood to do so with his wife of 17 years.

"You three head around to the back. Make sure that he doesn't try to go anywhere once we make our presence known. Damien, go with them," Charlie said. "The rest of y'all come with me. It's about time we teach Mr. Gillespie that when you make a deal, you have to live up to your end of the bargain."

Indeed, Mr. Gillespie had not held up his end of the deal. Had not even tried. He had entered into an arrangement with the bikers whereby they would take care of a small, minor issue with a business rival of his. It'd been a simple enough task; scare the living hell out of the guy and then tell him that he needed to back off from a particular housing development deal. Mr. Gillespie provided half of the money up front. The other half was supposed to be given to the club once the man had pulled out of the real estate deal. That had happened. The second payment had not. Now they were going to have a little talk to Mr. Gillespie in regards to his overdue account. The three remaining men and the three remaining wolves made their way up the driveway to the front of the house.

Bulldog broke off from the other two. He was accompanied by a biker brother in his full wolf form. Together, they went around side of the house where the patio door was located. Bulldog looked in through the window and saw Mr. Gillespie on the couch with a lovely woman dressed in nothing but a black lace and sequin teddy, sitting in his lap while he drank a beer and fondled her ample breasts. It was no secret that Gillespie had a hard time keeping his, if you believed the rumors, less than adequate cock in his pants. The young woman was his mistress and she was not the only one who was well kept by members of the state legislature in this particular neighborhood. The Annondale development was well known for being a place where the state's politicians kept their secrets and while she may have thought that she was special, the truth was, she was just another secret being kept in the shadows by a man who felt he could do so with impunity because of his power.

Bulldog looked down at his wolf brother and gave a slight nod. The wolf began to growl and bark loudly at the glass door. Mr. Gillespie jumped visibly as he cast his eyes toward the glass door. As soon as he saw the massive outlaw bikers, he immediately knew that things had taken a very serious turn for the worse and his plans for the evening were ruined. He frantically pushed the young lady off of his lap and stood up, heading toward the stairs, but it was too late. The front door had been forced open by the other two bikers and they cut Mr. Gillespie off in the foyer of the house. He turned his head toward the kitchen, hoping to make for the back door, but was met by Damien.

"Guys, seriously," Gillespie said with a nervous chuckle in his voice. "There's been a big misunderstanding. The money that I owe you, it got misdirected. It's going to be delivered to you very, very shortly, I swear."

"We're so glad to hear that, Gene. See, we were under the impression that perhaps you might have been stupid enough to think that you could scam us out of what we agreed on. Now, deep down, we know you can't be that stupid. Although the thought did cross our minds to the possibility, seeing as how you are a politician and all," Charlie said as he crossed his arms over his broad chest and looked squarely at Gillespie.

"I promise. It wasn't any type of scam or anything. I would never even think about trying to double cross you guys. I'm not that stupid, as you should know" Gillespie said, backing up a little bit more in the room, trying to center himself as far from the bikers as he could get. The outlaws were not moving to match him. They knew they had the upper hand. The six wolf companions had now made their way into the house as well and had taken up positions between that of the men. Gillespie wasn't going anywhere, that was certain.

"The problem is, Gene, now we have a serious trust issue between us. See, we're not sure that we can really believe what you're telling us because we are sincerely doubting whether or not you were honest in your original arrangements with us." Charlie said

"I promise you, guys. I'm going to get this straightened out. I'll get you the money that you're owed no later than 48 hours from now. I promise. Look, gentlemen, seriously, please be reasonable!" he said as he finally backed himself up to the point that his legs were touching the front of couch on which his mistress was still sitting.

"And why should we trust you, Gene?" Charlie asked.

"Yeah, why should we trust you? What's in it for us if we give you another chance to make this right?" Axel asked.

"Look, guys, I'm sure that we can work something out here. Some sort of interest rate or good-faith payment!" Gillespie said. He was now becoming more and more visibly disturbed by the fact that the situation did not appear to be going in his favor. He had known at the time that it was a stupid mistake to try to scam the bikers, but he was really regretting his decision now. He had been arrogant in thinking that because of who he was, he would simply be able to get away with it. He had heard rumors about them, about how they were, the things they did. He had thought that his position as a public figure would protect him. Now he could see that was folly on his part.

"It's a very interesting idea," Charlie said, "And you're right; we are owed some sort of consideration for the inconvenience of having you think we're stupid enough that you could pull the slip on us and get away with it. Make no mistake, Gillespie; we know that you tried to scam us out of our money. The only thing that is saving your skinny white ass is the fact that, at the moment, we know that it would be much more inconvenient for us to tear you into tiny little pieces and leave you scattered all over town then it would be for us to go ahead and trust you one more time to get this straight. And now is your chance to make good on your end of our deal. So here's how this is going to work. You have 24 hours to get us the money that's owed to us. If you do not, then we are going to track you down, and we're going to hurt you. We're going to hurt you very badly. But, before we do that, we are going to hurt your wife. We're going to hurt your children. We'll hurt your dog. Do you understand this?" Charlie asked. Gillespie could tell from the look of the man's eyes that he was deadly serious.

"As for the inconvenience that you've caused us, I am sure that we can think of something that you can do to make it up to us," Charlie said as he looked at the pretty blond sitting on the couch before him. He moved his hand down to his heavy crotch and gave his hefty manhood a firm squeeze.

"You have got to be kidding me. No." She said as he she jumped her feet and looked down at Gillespie. "They cannot be serious."

"You need to sit down and shut up before things get out of hand, little lady." Damien said.

"Oh, is that right, you son of a bitch? You think you can just walk in here with your damn dogs and take over the place and Gene is supposed to give into whatever extortion that you are trying to pull. I don't think so. This isn't a Hollywood movie. You guys need to get real," she said.

"I assure you, baby, they are more than real, and they wouldn't be here if they were not serious. Very serious. Just do what they want and it will be okay. Trust me," Gillespie said as he sat there with his head hung low.

He knew that the men were going to get what they wanted. Men like them always got what they wanted. The only thing that he had to accept now was that the tight perfect pussy that he had enjoyed fucking so many times over the last three years was going to be taken by the long, thick cocks of these brutish thugs. There was no way after this that he was ever going to be able to fuck her again. He wouldn't even want to after they had been inside of her and soiled her with their kind. He had let his pride come to this.

"No. I won't do it. You guys need to get out of my house right now and leave us alone or I'm calling the police and the dog catcher," the woman said, only half convincingly.

"Stacy, please, just sit down and shut up. These are not the kind of guys who you fuck with, okay? Just please shut up and do what they say, for the sake of us both! And, I hate to say it, but whatever they're going to do with you, you're going to enjoy it way more than you ever did with me," Gillespie said.

"The man's got a point. And you were right. This ain't no damn movie. This is very real and, like your boyfriend told you, we are not the kind of men that you fuck with. Now, he owes us and you're gonna pay the difference right now or I'm gonna go to the papers and then he can explain to the press what happened to you in this little love nest. And besides, as he said, you *will* enjoy being with us and you will be pleasured, beyond anything you've ever known. Have I made myself very clear?" For the first time since they entered the house, the woman was totally speechless. She looked up at Charlie and the others. Her eyes were focused on the enormous bulge at the front of his pants. She looked over at Gene.

"We're through," she said.

"That might be a good idea. But it doesn't change anything right now. The only thing that you have to choose now is, do we do this one at a time or do you want to get wild and take us all on at the same time?" Charlie said. She looked around the room.

"Let's go for one at a time. You are obviously the best-looking one, so I'll start with you!" she said looking up at Charlie.

"Naturally," He replied.

She stood up and looked at him with curious lust. She turned and looked at Gillespie with a more disgusted, hate filed look, "Oh, little man, you are so gonna pay for this!" she said.

"And I'm sure that he is going to deserve every minute of what he has coming to him. For now though, Damien, why don't you show the lady upstairs, where she can get more comfortable in the bedroom? I will be up shortly," Charlie said as the tall, thin biker with the long flowing black hair walked over and took her by the arm to escort her to the master bedroom upstairs. "Oh and Damien. I am first. You heard the lady."

"Sure thing, boss."

"As for you, Gene. You are going to sit here and be a good boy while we take care of this business we have with your woman. If you even think of trying anything stupid, we will either shoot you or let the wolves have you. Do you understand?" Charlie asked.

"Yes…yes I understand," he replied.

"Good. Not as stupid as we thought after all." Charlie said as he started to turn and leave the room to join the girl upstairs.

"Hey boss, I…I'll stand guard out in the side yard, okay?" Bulldog said.

"Bull, do you really think that is such a good idea, in light of the conversation we had the day before yesterday? This is a group activity. You might want to consider being a part of the group for a change. In fact, why don't you come with me; you can go second," Charlie said as Bulldog realized that it was less of a suggestion, but rather a flat out order. He was going to take part in the pleasuring of the girl and that was that. It didn't matter if he hated to fuck women or not. He had known he was completely gay since he was about 18 years old, but that didn't matter right now. Tonight, he was going to have sex with a woman. It was his orders and that meant it was his duty to the club. He walked out of the room with Charlie, looking as if he had just been told he was being escorted to a firing squad.

'Well, here goes nothing…' Bulldog thought to himself as they made their way up the stairs.

*****

"Hi! Where have you been, stud?" Steve asked as Bulldog walked in the door of the coffee house the next morning.

"Had to go out of town on club business. Glad to be back here though. Missed you. Sorry I couldn't tell you I was leaving, I didn't really know until about 10 minutes before we walked out the door of the clubhouse and by then it was too late. Once we are on a run to go do something, cellphones and personal calls are a major no-no. I will try in the future to not let it happen again. Sorry if I worried you," Bulldog said as he walked over to the counter.

"Well, you did. But I forgive you. You're too cute to stay mad at. Want your regular?" Steve asked.

"God, yes, I would love that. Do me a favor and make it two shots of espresso today though. I hardly got any sleep last night."

"Sure thing,' Steve said as he watched Bulldog lumber over to their normal table.

The big man did look exhausted. Hell, he looked dead on his feet. Steve slipped a third shot of espresso into the coffee to help perk him up. He didn't want to take a chance on him being out on the road on the bike and his mind not being 100% clear. Steve thought about what he was doing, taking care of this man, and why he felt compelled to do so, and suddenly found himself laughing a little to himself. He actually was starting to care about the big lug. He also hoped that what he had to ask him would help perk him up a bit. Steve finished making the coffees and gathering some biscuits and fixings and walked to the table to sit down with Bulldog.

"I hope it's a very long time before I have to go out on a mission like that again. Damn near wore me out, all the back and forth we did on the bikes over the past two days." Bulldog said.

"Well, you're back here now and you're safe and sound and really, that's all that matters. What is it you said the phrase was? Vertical…one piece, no holes. I'm glad for it," Steve said Bulldog looked at him and smiled.

"You really do listen to me when I talk, don't you?" Bulldog asked.

"Of course I do. I find you and your life interesting. Why would I not listen? It may come as a shock to you, but I actually care about you and your health. I want you to be safe, or as safe as you can be when you're out there doing the things that you have to get done for the club. I understand this is your life and that it means the world to you and I accept that it's dangerous and that there is nothing else to be done about that. Just be as careful as you can is all I ask."

Bulldog smiled and looked out the window. He felt warm inside just hearing that from Steve. He had never had anyone who had cared enough about him one way or the other to say anything like that. What made it even more special was that he could tell that Steve really meant it. He knew that his lifestyle was dangerous and while he wished it wasn't, he knew that it was a part of his life and accepted that, and all of the risk that went with it. For some reason, at that moment, when Bulldog felt so down on himself, at such a low point in his life, knowing that truth made things slightly better.

"I will do my best to stay safe. I promise," Bulldog said as he looked back over at Steve.

"Good. Now then, moving on to other things. I have a very important question. Since you had such a hard trip, how would you like to unwind at my place tonight? With a nice home cooked meal and a quiet evening for just the two of us?" Steve asked.

"That's sounds like a great idea. Exactly what I need. What time should I be there?" Bulldog asked.

"Seven would be great. I get off at 4:30 and that will give me time to get to the store and then get back and make dinner. Oh no, look who walked in. I'll be back. I have to go take care of something. I owe old Mr. Pritchard a comp from last time he was in and we totally messed up his order," Steve said as he got up and walked away from the table. Bulldog turned and just watched him work for a little while. There was a gentle comfort in that. He could not explain why but there was.

*****

"Bulldog!" Charlie yelled out across the crowded clubhouse. Bulldog turned and looked at him. The last thing that he wanted to deal with right now was another deep and meaningful talk with the pack and club leader. He knew Charlie would have nothing good to say to him. He thought for a moment about trying to make a quick dart for the door and escape but he knew that eventually he would get cornered and then it would just be worse. Charlie made his way across the room to where he was standing.

"What's up, man?" Bulldog said.

"I just wanted to come over and say that I have noticed a new attitude with you the last couple of weeks and that the whole thing that went down in Birmingham, well, I hope you know that was just for the benefit of the guys. I wanted them to see what I had already started to see, that you were on the mend with all of that other crap that you had been going through." Charlie said.

"I understand, boss. No big deal. Hell, I have to admit, I did have fun." Bulldog replied, hoping Charlie couldn't spot the lie.

"See, that's what I'm talking about. That's what this life is about, ain't it? Getting shit done and, in the end, having fun. So, anyway, that's it. I did want to ask what it was that caused the change in your thinking and acting, though. Got me curious," Charlie asked.

"Can't really say, boss. Just have had some stuff that has been going my way, finally. Feeling better on some things. Guess it's got my head back in the right place."

"Well, whatever it is, keep it up, brother. It's nice to see the old you again," Charlie said as he slapped Bulldog's back hard and then turned and walked away. A moment later Axel came walking up with a beer in his hand and a big smile on his face.

"Hey, man. I was wondering if you might want to go out for a run with me tonight. Just the two of us, like we used to. Get out there and just run the woods for a few hours to blow off some steam. What do you say?" Axel said.

"I would love to, brother, but I just can't tonight. I already have plans that I just can't break. I tell you what though, why don't we try to do it either tomorrow night or Sunday? Sunday would be great, if you want to," Bulldog said as he playfully punched Axel on the shoulder as he turned to walk out the door of the clubhouse.

"Yeah, sure. I understand. Sunday, then. We'll try for Sunday," Axel said. He had never in his wildest dreams thought that his best friend would just blow him off for other 'plans'. Him and Bulldog went back ages and he could always count on him for a good run. He was going to find out what was behind this new attitude that Bulldog had and why he was spending so much time doing his own thing recently, and he resolved to find out that night.

****

Bulldog stopped by the mall on his way home and bought a new outfit, realizing that if he showed up wearing the same one that he had been wearing when they went out on their first date, he would look beyond pathetic. He tried his best to find something that looked nice, though shopping was not really his favorite activity. He could only hope that when he put it on, he wouldn't look too much like either a dork or a dumbass. He finally found something that he thought didn't look half bad, bought it, and decided to hurry home. He was halfway home when he looked at his watch and saw that he only had a couple of hours left before he was supposed to be at Steve's house. He hightailed it home to get cleaned up and changed.

After going through his routine of getting ready, he took one last look in the mirror. 'Not bad. Not bad at all,' he thought to himself with a smile.

Bulldog arrived at the front door of Steve's house right at 7, on the dot. He had a bottle of wine in his hand and felt an excitement that he hadn't felt in a very long time. He was so glad that not only had Steve forgiven him for his behavior on their first date and decided to give him another chance, but that he had been so understanding and had come up with the idea for their next date to be in the privacy of their own homes. He felt a lot more comfortable than he had been when they were going out to a restaurant that just wasn't him or his style. Here, at Steve's house, with nobody else around, he felt he could truly be himself. He pressed the doorbell and soon was face to face with the incredible man that he had the pleasure of spending the evening with once more.

"Hey you. Come on in," Steve said as he ushered Bulldog into the house.

"I wasn't sure what, if anything, to bring so I just brought this. Sorry if it's wrong," Bulldog said handing the gift-wrapped bottle of wine to Steve. Steve opened the package and looked at the bottle.

"Wow, this is a very nice wine, Lucas. Thank you. You did a good job. You didn't have to do that though," The big man blushed as he looked down at the floor and kicked his shoe around a little, moving an imaginary something on the carpet for lack of knowing what better to do with himself.

"Well, sit down, make yourself comfortable. I am just finishing up with dinner. If you want to come into the kitchen and keep me company, that'd be great. Or you can plop down in the living room, relax, and catch part of the game. Your choice."

Bulldog thought about it for as second and while he would be more comfortable sitting and watching the game, there was a part of him that told him that was not the right choice among the options. Plus, any chance to spend a little extra time staring at Steve was always a good option in his book.

"Sure, I'll come in there with you. Sounds like a better choice to me. Might be able to give you a hand, though I don't know with what. But I'll try with whatever help you may need," he said as he started to follow Steve through the house to the kitchen.

"I don't need a thing from you except your charming company. Just sit there at the breakfast bar and have a beer, if you want. I got some craft beers for you at the store. I remembered last time you said you liked the Irish Red and I went to four stores before I finally found it," Steve said with a wink as he went back to working on the large pot that was on the stove.

"Oh, you didn't have to go to all of that trouble," Bulldog said.

"Sure I did. I wanted to make tonight special. Now, like I said, you sit there and tell me about your trip. Or as much of it as you can tell."

Bulldog was firstly impressed that Steve actually wanted to know about what it is that he did and secondly that he understood that there were things about his life that he would not be able to share with him. Of course, Steve had no idea that there was a very important part of Bulldog's life that he could not share with him, but for reasons that had nothing to do with the patch that he wore on his back. While Steve finished up the cooking, Bulldog talked as much as he could about the trip that the club had taken to Birmingham. Eventually the conversation moved on to other aspects of the city, including the fact that before Steve took the job at Joe's, he had almost taken a similar position in a city much further away.

"Well, I am most certainly glad that you decided on Joe's," Bulldog said as he helped carry the last couple of dishes to the table.

"I am too," Steve said turning around and smiling at Bulldog as he sat the entree down in the center of the table.

"I don't have any idea what this all is but it looks incredible and it smells even better," Bulldog said.

"Well, my family on my mother's side is Greek so I thought, why not make a Greek feast. I'll explain things as we go along, but for now, just sit there and make yourself comfortable and let's eat," Steve said.

Bulldog had never had Greek food before but he was very impressed, both with the recipes and with the skills at which Steve had prepared them. He was an instant fan of the cuisine and with Steve's cookery. At the end of the meal, he made a special effort to tell him that he hoped that he had more chances to enjoy his cooking in the future.

"I'm sure there will be lots of opportunities, BD. Now, I have one more surprise. Come on out to the beck deck. I have the fire pit set up and figured we could look at the stars and chat some more. Grab a couple of more beers if you want," Bulldog could not believe that Steve really was this amazing and sweet. He seemed too good to be true. Bulldog found himself growing more and more interested in him by the minute.

As they sat on the deck looking up at the stars, both of the men felt strangely and wonderfully at peace. They talked idly about things that were of no particular importance, but it was nice to be able to freely chat with an understanding partner. Just looking at the fire and enjoying each other's company. After a while, Steve's hand slowly moved over to the side and his fingers started to lightly graze Bulldog's hand. Bulldog looked down and saw what he was doing and suddenly a new feeling started to form inside of him. The feeling of contentment that he had desired for such a long time.

He suddenly realized what it was that he had been missing in his life. The thing that he had been searching for to fill that indescribable void in his being. He was looking for love and he felt as though, at that very moment, that he might be sitting beside the man that could give him that love. He moved his hand slightly and let his own fingers start to lightly graze those of Steve in return. Soon their hands were intertwined. Bulldog had a desire that he could not control. He moved his body up and turned to Steve. The two men locked eyes with each other. Both knew that they wanted the other, but both felt scared. They had both been hurt in so many different ways, so many times, that they were afraid to let their souls open up. The two of them moved ever so closer to each other at slow, deliberate pace. Eventually, their lips finally touched and in that instant they both felt as if the power flowing between them made them whole for the first time in their lives.

In that moment, Bulldog suddenly felt as if everything was right in his world. He didn't care about the stresses and disagreements with the club. He forgot about being a werewolf and the fears and anxieties that came with trying to hide his secret. He forgot about how much he hated the town and most of the backwoods redneck dumbasses that lived there. For a moment, he felt human, normal, alive, and happy. He felt happy for the first time in as long as he could remember.

Steve also felt like he was no longer utterly alone in the world. He felt as if he was filled with life, filled with a reason to live once more. He forgot about the duel betrayal of his lover and his best friend. He forgot about how hard it had been to walk away from almost everything that he had and had worked for, in order to start fresh. He forgot about the pain that he had felt and the fear that he would spend the rest of his life alone. For a moment, he too felt invigorated, normal, alive, and happy.

The kiss grew deeper and both men started to stand as they began to let their hands roam around each other's body, the first truly intimate touching that they had shared in the nearly two months that they had known each other.

"I want you, Lucas. I need you," Steve said as he reached up and started to unfasten the buttons on Bulldogs shirt.

As he pulled the front of the shirt open and yanked the tails of it form the big man's waistband, he looked at the massive expanse of the wide barrel chest under the bright white of the cotton crewneck undershirt the big biker stud was wearing underneath. He could see the vague outlines of the big bear's tattoos on his skin through the thin white fabric. He could also see the shadows of the man's thick forest of dark brown chest hair as well. He moved his fingertip to Bulldog's chest and started to lightly trace the lines of the tattoos. The sensation of Steve's touch was electric to Bulldog and he closed his eyes and savored it. He gripped lightly at the back of Steve as he let the feeling of passion and desire that he was feeling flow over him and fill his very being.

"I want you too, Steve. I have since the first day I saw you." Bulldog pulled his shirt off from his body and let it drop to the surface of the deck. Next he yanked the tails of his undershirt form his waist and pulled it over his head, throwing it down to the ground with his other shirt. The exposure of his massive hairy body, covered in art and packed with hard firm muscle, was almost too much for Steve to be able to bear. Steve took the cue and also stripped to the waist. Upon seeing that Bulldog had his nipples pierced, Steve moved his head close to the hairy chest of the biker stud and began to suck his pierced nipples. Licking the barbell piercings that were there, occasionally chewing lightly at the hard nipples, Steve moaned as he felt Bulldog's warm skin inside his mouth for the first time. Steve noticed something else that was growing stiff in Bulldog's pants and Steve's hand moved down to inspect it, as he gripped lightly at Bulldog's crotch. Not wanting to scare Steve away too quickly, Bulldog gently moved Steve's hand away and gripped it in his own as he maneuvered his face to begin kissing Steve once more.

"I need to tell you something. I am, well, very large. Without a doubt, larger than any man you have ever been with or even seen before. And I'm not just saying that. I don't want you to be scared when you see it," Bulldog said.

"Lucas, I can tell you're large just by looking at you. I have seen that bulge in your jeans before," Steve replied with a wry grin.

"No, it's different. I normally wear a very tight jockstrap to keep it all in. When I say I'm very large, I mean…" and he moved his hand back to his crotch and let Steve feel the swelling manhood that was there. Steve's eyes got wide.

"You mean, absolutely huge," Steve said.

"Yeah, exactly. Is that a problem?" Bulldog asked.

"Are you kidding? Not at all. Never had a man as big as you, but I want you, more than anything. Let's just start slow though, okay?" Steve said breathlessly into Bulldog's chest as he slowly lowered himself to his knees before the powerful and large biker bear. He reached up and started to unfasten Bulldog's thick, leather belt. The biker took a deep breath. His heart was racing. This was the moment that he had been waiting for since he had first seen Steve in the coffee house. He had also been dreading this moment. When most people saw his enormous cock, they either freaked out or couldn't control themselves and wanted nothing but sex from that point forward. He wanted more than just a physical relationship with Steve, however. This was quite possibly the guy that he had been waiting his whole life for, he felt. The one that he might consider growing old with. He didn't want Steve's desire to turn into something less.

Steve slipped Bulldog's pants down off of his hips to his knees. As he did, he looked up and saw the massive bulge in the front of the big man's underwear. He could not believe the immense size of it, but now he could understand why Bulldog had been so self-conscious about exposing himself. It had to be difficult to live with something that large, as nice as it was to have it. He was determined, however, to make sure that Bulldog didn't feel self-conscious for long. He reached up and cradled the swelling bulge with his hand as Bulldog looked down at him. He moved up and took ahold of the waistband of the big biker's underpants and slid them down his long, hairy legs. As he did, the largest piece of manhood that he had ever seen came out into the open.

"My god…" he said as he looked up at Bulldog and smiled. "You are a big one, it's true. But it's beautiful, Lucas. But it's not who you are. I want it, but only because it's attached to you."

Those words were, without a doubt, the most wonderful thing that Bulldog had ever heard in his life. Steve moved his hand up to the incredible hunk of flesh that was before him. It was swelling more rapidly, now that the anxiety and excitement of it being exposed had left Bulldog's mind. Steve leaned forward and started to slowly lick at the tip of the thick pole that was lying across the palm of his hand. He had fantasized about this moment and he knew that Bulldog was large but he never in his wildest imagination thought that he would be about to try to suck such a huge, rock-hard cock.

He slowly pulled back the biker studs foreskin to expose his cock head. It was smooth, shiny with his natural oils, and reddish purple in color. It was the most delightful cock head he had ever seen on a man. Steve had never touched an uncut man before and he was a little concerned that he might cause the big guy some discomfort if he was not careful with his actions. Bulldog didn't seem to mind though. He actually let out a slight moan as he felt his skin being retracted. Steve started to lick the underside of Bulldog's cock, the tip of his tongue playing gently with the tight band of nerves under his cockhead. It was a pleasurable sensation for any man but when the surface of Steve's tongue touched the delicate nerve cluster on Bulldog's cock, the big biker almost jumped twenty feet in the air. He felt his body surge with the power of his wolf side trying to break through as the passion of the moment took him over. He gripped lightly on Steve's shoulders, who mistook the action for a desire for him to go forward with his endeavors. He opened his mouth as wide as he could and let the huge cock slip inside.

"My God!" Bulldog said as he fought the urge to change even partially. He couldn't let his wolf side come out, not even for a second. The pleasure he was feeling was overloading every part of his being and making it damn near impossible for him to keep himself under control. He soon had his composure back, however, as he grew accustomed to the pleasurable feeling of Steve's mouth on his massive cock.

Steve was doing his best to suck Bulldog as well as he could, but there was just so much cock to deal with that he was having a hard time getting more than five or six inches of it into his mouth. He even tried to deep throat the head, but he found it almost impossible to get it past the opening of his throat. He used his hands to work on the big low balls of the bear brute above him as they hung low in Bulldog's sack. He also used his other hand on the shaft of the warm, big prick. Bulldog wasn't complaining at all. He had never had anyone try so hard to suck him completely before and he was flattered at the effort. He was actually enjoying the sensations that were happening to him, and he thought his moans of delight would convey those emotions. Soon, however, Steve pulled off and stood up.

"This isn't working, I can't believe I'm gonna say it, but it's too big! I love it. I am going to have to practice using my mouth on that thing, but I know one place that it will fit. My ex used to fist me, so I'm used to having large things inside of me," he said as he kicked off his loafers and unbuttoned his pants. Underneath he was wearing a pair of grey boxer-briefs that showed off his legs and package very well. They didn't do a thing to hide the rock hard erection that Steve had though. He tossed the pants to the side and slipped his underwear off, letting them drop to the ground.

Bulldog was also busy pulling his hiking boots off and stripping out of his pants and underwear. "Be right back," Steve called as he disappeared into the house and came back a few moments later with the bottle of silicone lube from his nightstand. He tossed the bottle to Bulldog, who caught it in midair. He looked at the bottle and smiled.

"Good idea," he said, "Sometimes lube is just the right thing to do." He chuckled as he started to wet his cock with the slick gel. Steve got up onto the patio table and lifted his legs so that the big man could start to lube his hole while he stroked his large cock with his free hand to make sure that it was well coated. This wasn't just some random person the wolf brothers fucked in the woods before a feast, this was a man that Bulldog cared about, very deeply, and he wanted to make sure that he made this as gentle and pleasurable on him as possible the first time. "You ready?" He asked.

"As ready as I am ever going to be, I suppose. Just go easy on me at first, okay?" Steve said.

"You got it. Don't even worry. Just relax and enjoy." Bulldog said as he lined up with the tight pink hole of Steve. He pressed the massive end of his now very slick cock to Steve's open hole as he reached down and took one of Steve's hands into his own grip as a loving gesture of comfort. The two men looked into each other eyes as Bulldog gave a hard shove and his knob entered Steve, who let out a loud grunt of pleasure as he was penetrated. Bulldog was very gentle as he slowly worked his cock into Steve's hole. He took his time but stopped when he only had half of it inside of the other man.

"What's wrong?" Steve said as he grunted through the ecstasy that he felt form being stretched so much by the big dick of his biker buddy.

"Nothing, just giving you a break. Letting you enjoy it all. Gonna fuck nice and easy. In and out now, with only half of it, until you get used to me," he said as he pulled back a little and added more lube to his cock shaft. He gave a hard push and easily slid back inside. Steve let out another moan of pleasure and asked for more. Another stroke brought about still more pleasure this time. Then another, and another. Soon, Bulldog was able to use a steady pace with his thrusts and was slowly pushing more and more of his nearly footling cock into Steve upon each entry.

For the next few minutes, the men engaged in their steamy act of lust and desire. Bulldog was feeling his own powerful wolf needs starting to take ahold of him, but he held back as much as he could. Suddenly, after Steve moaned Bulldog's name, the feeling started to grow. The feeling that that he had felt so many times before, and had been trying to hide all night. His dominant, powerful side. The side that was fueled by the drives of his wild wolf essence was starting to come to the forefront. He knew that with what he was feeling, he would not be able to control himself. He knew that the desire to breed was too strong for him to control. He would never be able to pull himself out. But he also could not allow himself to breed Steve. He didn't want to turn Steve into a half-wolf. He didn't want another man to have to live the way that he lived, to fight the battles that he had to fight. He suddenly pulled out of Steve's hole and stepped back.

"Stop, wait. We need to stop. I'm sorry but I can't do this right now. I'm so sorry." Bulldog said as he pushed Steve's backside way from his crotch.

"Is there something wrong? Did I do something that you didn't like, Lucas?" Steve asked.

"No, it's not anything like that, I swear. It was great. You were great. It's me. I just have…well, it's just been a very long time and I have some stuff I need to work through. I loved what you were doing, but I know that if I let you keep going, that it's going to lead to more than you know right now and I'm not ready for that yet. I promise I will be soon, but please understand, I can't make love to you right now, no matter how much I want to," Bulldog said as he laid back and closed his eyes, feeling like a world-class jerk for ruining a perfect moment between the two of them, for not being able to tell Steve the entire truth.

Steve could tell that Bulldog was torn up about having to stop what they were doing. He understood there was more to the story than Bulldog was letting on. He wasn't going to make things worse by asking a lot of questions or pressure him in any way.

"Its okay, big man. If you're not ready to take things to that level, then I won't pressure you. We will wait and, when you are ready, then it will be that much better, okay? It's all right, Lucas. I just want to spend time with you and see what happens," Steve said.

"I just want you to know that I want to. I want you. I really want to. Just know that it's not anything to do with you, okay? The problem is me, " Bulldog said.

"It doesn't matter. It's okay. We will work it out, whatever it is. I'm not letting you go that easily. We will just wait until you are ready and, until then, we will just cuddle and kiss, and be with each other. Is that okay?" Steve asked. Bulldog pulled him close to his chest and wondered how he had gotten so lucky as to find a guy who was so incredible and understanding.

Steve felt disappointed by the sudden stoppage of the activity but, at the same time, he was content to just lay there under the stars, with the massive arms of the big biker wrapped around him and their naked bodies pressed against each other. He looked up at the twinkling heavens and wondered how he could have gotten so lucky as to be have such a great guy feel for him the way that Bulldog felt for him.

Bulldog looked up at the heavens and felt the same way, but at the same time, his heart was heavy. He thought about how close things had just gotten. He had allowed himself a moment of weakness. He had allowed himself to think for a few minutes that he was a normal human being and that he could just make love to man he cared so much about and that there would be no consequences. He could not believe that he had almost been so careless. He held Steve close to him. He knew that he would have to deal with this eventually but he had no earthly idea how he could without making thing awkward between them or worse, without Steve leaving. He was too big to use a condom and, even if he wasn't, he didn't want to give Steve the wrong idea. The whole excuse of 'we should be safe at first' would only work for so long before Steve would want them to do it without anything between them. Bulldog had a big problem and he had no idea where to even start to work out how to get around it. He had to tell Steve the complete truth, but he didn't know how.

Of course, as Bulldog lay there holding Steve and getting lost with him in the heavens above them, he was happy. He was with the man he loved and he felt that Steve truly loved him as well. However, laying there, feeling the cool night air on their naked flesh, they had no idea exactly how much of a problem they really had. Deep in the shadows of the trees behind the house, a pair of eyes was looking at them. Deep, red eyes. The eyes of a turned wolf.

Axel had been there the entire night, in his wolf form. Watching, listening, waiting to see how far this would go, and trying to decide what to do about it. Deep down, he knew that there was only one thing that he could do. He took an oath to the club, to the pack, and he had to do his duty to protect the pack from anything that may threaten it. He had to do his duty, even if that may mean that he had to hurt his best friend, to protect him from himself. He had only one choice. He turned and ran into the night.

*****

# Volume Four – The Choice

Bulldog walked into the clubhouse. Most of the guys were there and as he looked around at them, something strange happened in his mind. He realized that while he felt more like himself, more connected to who he was for the first time in a very long time, he didn't feel any more connected to the club. He didn't feel anything for the men that he had called brothers for the past seven years. He still felt a small connection to them as a wolf pack but even that was weak and fleeting. At that very moment, he realized another important for why he had been so miserable for so long. He was living a life that was not what he wanted it to be. He loved being a biker; he loved the life that he had chosen for himself. He loved the lifestyle itself but not the way that he had been living it. He saw that now. The outlaw life was not for him anymore.

He supposed that at one time, when he first joined the club, he needed that crazy lifestyle. But now it was something that was no longer a vital part of him, if any part at all. He had even started to wonder if it was the club that he desired when he joined or if it was the other part of it, the pack. He was as young and as green as they came back then. He was looking for someone to show him the way and these guys came out and gave him a path to follow, a life to make his own. They gave him brotherhood, family, purpose and, most of all, a safe place where he could be accepted for what he was and not have to hide it. He had learned how to be a wolf in the pack that they offered, but at the same time, they had taught him to be a man that he was not really happy being anymore. He didn't want to be a thug, a criminal, or an outlaw. He wanted to just be a normal biker, loving his freedom and his life the way that he wanted it to be.

"Bulldog, can I see you for a minute? We need to talk about something that's kind of important," Charlie said as he walked across the room and put his hand on Bulldog's shoulder and led him back toward the chapel, the room where they held their executive meetings and decided the things needed to be decided for the day-to-day operations of the club. Bulldog could tell that whatever it was that Charlie wanted to talk to him about, it was not something that he was going to particularly enjoy discussing. They walked into the chapel room and Charlie closed the door behind them.

"Have a seat brother. Make yourself comfortable," Charlie said.

"I would prefer to stand, if that is okay?" Bulldog said. He did not like the way that this was going already and the feeling was getting more and more intense as the seconds ticked by.

"Suit yourself," Charlie said as he moved one of the chairs aside and sat on the edge of the table with one hip. He looked over to the wall where there hung a banner that had been made by a couple of the club workers years earlier. The banner read 'Brotherhood Is Everything. Pack First, Club Second. There Is No Third!'

"You know that banner has hung there for a very long time. The people who made it were among the most loyal that this club had ever had. When they were put down, it was a damn shame, but things got out of hand one night and during a moon party they got caught up in the fray. One of them got bred, the other one got bitten…anyways, it doesn't matter how it happened. They were infected. Had to take them out. Both were females and weak. They would have never made the change even if we had let them live. They would have suffered terribly. They made that banner for this room only a couple of months before that happened. I am sure, even as we were putting them down, showing them mercy, they thought about it. They knew what this club was and they served our pack well. They were committed."

"What's this all about, Boss?" Bulldog asked.

"I am just wondering if you understand that commitment, Bull."

"What are you talking about? I have been committed to this club for more than seven years. This pack is my family," Bulldog said, only half meaning the statement and wondering if Charlie could tell that.

"Yeah, you have, for the most part. But I have to wonder if you are still committed. See, there are some things that have come to my knowledge, disturbing things that have upset me, worried me and I have to ask you about them," Charlie said as he took out a cigarette and lit it. He didn't bother to offer one to Bulldog, as he knew the man didn't smoke.

"What things?" Bulldog asked hesitantly.

"I have been told that there is a new love interest in your life. That you have been hanging out with someone. Well, no, more than hanging out. Let's call it what it is. Dating and fucking a full human, a male human, and that you have been doing this openly. Now, I need to ask you if that is true."

"So what if it is? I am not doing anything to damage the image of this club. When we went out in public, it was to a restaurant that is more than 40 miles from here and I was not wearing any colors. I was dressed citizen," Bulldog explained. "The rest of the time we just hang out at the coffee house and talk."

"From what I have been told, what you were doing the other night was a lot more than talking. I heard it to be that there was a lot of moaning and grunting going on and that you were stupid enough to be fucking this guy, knowing what could happen if you were to let things go too far. You know that we could not allow that, right? You know that this is wrong. It's against the rules and it puts us all at risk," Charlie said as he stood up and turned to face Bulldog head on.

"So, what, I'm not supposed to be happy because of this club and what we are? I love this man. I have, for the most part, gone along with everything that this pack has ever asked of me. I am looking for one thing that I can have that makes me happy and now you're telling me that it's against the rules. Bullshit!" Bulldog said.

"No, not bullshit. You know the rules. We don't get hooked up with outsiders. We don't get into relationships. Not as long as that patch is on your back. Have you thought about how dangerous this is for him? Being connected to you with the life that you lead here? Forget the risk of you accidently turning him. What could happen from that? What if he doesn't survive the change? Let's look beyond that. What about the life that we live, the things that go down, the messed up things we are forced to do all of the time? It puts him at risk just being associated with you and that puts us at risk as well. When does he start asking questions that you can't answer? Or will you answer them, Bull? Will you answer those questions while you have that anaconda of yours shoved up his backside, or is it the other way around now? Are you bending over for him and letting him breed your ass like a little girl?" Charlie said.

Bulldog reared back his fist and then stopped, biting his lip with his teeth so hard that he started to draw blood. His eyes shifted to their deep yellow color as he fought the fire inside of him that would lead to his shifting form. He knew that if he did, it would be a fight to the finish and he was not ready for that. Not yet, at least.

"That's right, Bull, back it down. Be smart. You haven't been very smart in this whole thing so far," Charlie said. "So here is how this goes. You go and you end this thing with this guy and then you come back here and we forget about this. No one except you and I ever has to know."

"And the person who told you like a fucking little ass weasel," Bulldog said.

"That's fair. You, I, and the aforementioned little ass weasel, who right now I trust, in terms of the loyalty of this club, a hell of a lot more than I trust you, that's for damn sure," Charlie said.

"Well, that's about where it stands then, ain't it?" Bulldog said.

"Yeah. It's real simple. You either end it with this guy or we will end it for you. I don't want it to come down to that."

"For your sake and the sake of the rest of the men in this club, I don't either" Bulldog replied.

"What's that supposed to mean?"

"It means, try anything toward Steve, even one little thing, and you'll be the first to find out," Bulldog said as he walked out of the room and stormed out of the clubhouse.

*****

"Hey! Come on in. I wasn't expecting to see you this afternoon," Steve said as he opened the door and let Bulldog into the house. He immediately noticed that there was something wrong.

"Yeah, I need to talk to you about something. It's kind of important. Do you have a few minutes?" Bulldog asked as he headed to the kitchen. Steve followed behind him, wondering what could be such an issue. When he got to the kitchen, he found Bulldog with the refrigerator door open, taking out one of the beers that Steve had bought for him for their romantic dinner the night before.

"Lucas, what is going on?" Steve asked. The sound of his real name was always something that had grated on his nerves but for some reason when it came off of the lips of Steve, it was almost angelic sounding.

"I just left the club. One of my so-called brothers has been spying on me. He went back and reported to the club president everything that I have been doing with you, including the most intimate details of our tryst last night on the back deck," he said as matter-of-factly as he could before taking a big swig of the beer while standing at the island counter.

"What?! You have got to be shitting me. They were spying on my house?" Steve said.

"Yeah, watching everything that we were doing the whole night, apparently up to and including while I was fucking you, or at least making the attempt to have sex with you, before I went all weird in the head and stopped everything."

"No, baby, you were fine. You had your reasons and I understand that. What I don't understand are guys from your club sitting behind my house and spying on what we were doing. Why would they do that? Steve asked.

"Because they think that me seeing you is a risk to the club and to the safety of our secrets. They think that they are protecting me and the club." Bulldog explained.

"What kind of right do they have to do that though? This is my home. They have no right to invade my privacy. And what secrets?" Steve said outraged. He could not believe that what should have been a private and intimate moment between them had been the source of potential entertainment by his friends. He wasn't mad at Bulldog. He knew that he didn't have anything to do with it. He was mad at them, but he knew that deep down there wasn't a damn thing that he could do about it. The only person who had any chance of making it right and putting them in their place was Bulldog and he had to trust that he would take care of it.

"I know. I'm sorry, I really am. I'm furious and I almost went after Charlie when he confronted me about our relationship. That and telling him that it was none of his business who I did what with," Bulldog said. Steve walked over to the fridge and took a beer out for himself, despite the fact that he was normally a wine only kind of guy. He handed a second one to Bulldog, as he could tell that the big man needed it.

"What did he say?" Steve asked as he popped the cap on the beer and took a big swig from it.

"He basically told me that dating you was against the rules of the club and that I had to break it off. His exact words were either I end it or they would." Suddenly the realization of how stupid it was for him to have told Steve that part hit him.

"What does that mean?" Steve asked quietly.

"It doesn't mean anything. The reason it doesn't is because you have me and I will protect you," Bulldog said as he came around the counter and put his hands on Steve's shoulders. "You listen to me. I have found a part of myself in you that I have been looking a long time to find. I am so glad that I have found you and I am not, I repeat, I am not letting you go that easy. I lo..." he stopped himself and Steve looked up at him suddenly, shocked at the phrase that he had almost said. From deep down inside, Bulldog summoned the courage to go on, "I love you, Steve."

Steve was speechless as he heard the words. Not because he was upset by them but because he was relieved that he had heard from Bulldog's mouth the same thing that he had been feeling for some time in his own heart. "I love you too, Lucas." He tilted his head back and Bulldog moved down and started to kiss him passionately on the mouth. For several minutes they kissed and then Bulldog broke the embrace and looked Steve in the eyes.

"I want you to know that I am here for the long haul, no matter what it takes. I have to go out for a few minutes but I will be right back. Why don't you whip up something simple for a lunch and then there is something that I want to talk to you about. I have a surprise for you when I get back," he said.

"Sure thing. Just be careful and don't be gone too long. If they are this upset, who knows what they will do..." Steve said.

"Baby, don't you worry about that. They won't try anything, not right now. They think I am here breaking up with you. The real drama won't start until after I talk to them tomorrow night during the club meeting. For now, just know that as long as I have anything to say about it, you are safe. Don't worry. I will take care of you," Bulldog said as he turned and walked out of the house. Steve could only hope that everything he had just said was true.

After Bulldog returned to Steve's house and they had lunch, spending the entire time talking about the situation and how they were going to deal with it, the big biker took Steve's hand and led him to the living room.

"I have something I want to tell you. I have been thinking about this for a long time and I have decided that if I have to make the choice between being with you and the club, then I choose you, Steve. At the club meeting tomorrow night, I am going to tell the guys that I am out. I'm turning in my colors and I want you and I to leave this place and go somewhere that we can be together. It's not going to be easy. There are things about me that I am still afraid to share with you, but I know that I want to share them when the time is right. For now I just want us to be together for the rest of our lives and the only way I can make that happen is to leave the club behind and start fresh," Bulldog said.

"But Lucas, you love being a biker. You can't just walk away from that," Steve said.

"No one said anything about not being a biker. I just don't want to be a part of the club anymore. I don't want to be an outlaw anymore. I want to go lone wolf," Bulldog said.

"What does that mean?" Steve asked.

"It means I am going at it by myself, without a club. Living my life, my way, without the rules and obligations of the club environment. It also means that I do not have to deal with being a part of the risky and dangerous stuff anymore. I don't want to do anything illegal or things of questionable morals anymore. I just want to love you and live straight and clean," Bulldog said.

"Baby, are you sure about this?" Steve asked.

"More sure about this than I have been about anything in my life. I just hope that once you learn the rest somewhere down the line, that you are able to live with it," he said.

"Lucas, whatever it is, no matter how bad or weird or difficult, we will make it work. I feel that I have spent my whole life waiting for a man like you and I won't let you go, no matter what," Steve replied.

"Okay, good. For now though, there is something that I want to do that I can't wait any longer for. I need you. I want to be with you, fully. But there is a reason we need to take precautions. I can't really explain everything right now, and this is going to sound completely absurd, but you have to believe me, okay? You must know that there is a genetic anomaly within me that means that when we have sex, we have to use protection. It's not a disease or anything like that. It's just, not something I can fully explain right now. But you have to know that I would never do anything to put you in danger. I will explain everything as soon as the time is right. I got these when I went out earlier. I am ready to make this commitment if you are," Bulldog said as he opened the bag and took out a box of double extra-large condoms. He laid them on the table in front of Steve.

"This anomaly, is it dangerous to me?" Steve asked.

"Not really dangerous per-se but it could be life altering in the right conditions. That's why I needed to stop the other night. There is a chance that I could pass the genetic anomaly on to you and if that were to happen, life could be difficult for you. I really can't explain more than that right now. It's not some horrible disease but it's a thing that I have to live with and I don't want to take the chance of you getting it," Bulldog explained.

"But you can't tell me more about it till later?" Steve asked.

"I have to ask you to trust me, Steve. I promise I will explain when I can, but there are reasons, club reasons, that I can't go into right now until after I do what I have to do with them and get them away from us for good. Once they are out of my life, I will be able to explain everything to you, but for now please know I love you and you can trust me."

There was something about Bulldog's eyes that told Steve that he was telling the truth and that he could trust him. He wasn't sure what was going on but he knew that he wanted to be with this man for the rest of his life and if that meant that he had to accept this genetic thing, whatever it was, then that was what he had to do and they would use protection for as long as was needed so they could be together.

"If you don't want to be with me, then I understand. This is a big step and I know it's a lot to ask you to trust me on this."

"Okay. I trust you and I want to be with you, Lucas. So is kissing okay still?" he said.

"Yes, of course, just as long as you don't have any open sores in your mouth. Eventually I will know more about whether you are even susceptible to the anomaly. Many people aren't but until then, it's better to play it safe."

"I understand. We will use protection and be safe, but for now I just want to be with you," Steve said as he moved forward and took Bulldog in his arms and began to passionately kiss him. For the next few minutes the two of them kissed and allowed their hands to roam over each other's bodies. The passion that they felt now, after sharing their deep, true feelings for each other was consuming them.

"Let's get upstairs and get all these clothes off. I want to feel your body against mine right now!" Bulldog said as he pulled Steve to his feet and led him upstairs to the bedroom.

They started to strip off their clothes and soon both men were naked. Once more Steve looked at the giant slab of man meat that was between the legs of the big biker brute that had stolen his heart. He looked at the broad hairy body of the big man and knew that it was his destiny to be with him. His looked into his eyes and knew that he was meant to be lost in them. He moved across the room and once again embraced Bulldog continuing the kiss that they had shared downstairs as the big man cupped his hands under Steve's ass and lifted him up, carrying him to the bed without breaking the kiss. He laid Steve down carefully and climbed onto the mattress himself.

"I love you, Lucas…" Steve said as he reached down and slowly and gently stroked the big man's massive member with his hand. The sensation was incredible and filled Bulldog with a renewed fire. He pulled Steve closer to him and kissed him deeper and more intensely than ever.

"I love you too. Are you sure that you are okay with this, baby?" Bulldog asked.

"Yes! I want you and I am okay with the risk. Give me that," Steve said as Bulldog moved his tool closer to his face. At the same time, Bulldog was opening one of the double extra-large condoms that he had bought. He wasn't even sure if they were going to fit, but he knew that he had to try. He wanted to be intimate with the man that he loved but he knew that he could not take the chance on turning him. He had to try one way or another. He stretched the opening as wide as he could and fit it over his engorged head, rolling it down his shaft carefully to avoid ripping it. Bulldog applied as much lube to himself as he could and then lifted Steve's legs.

"Okay, I'm ready. Are you?" he asked.

"Yep. I want to take you all. I want to feel all of you inside me. Just go slowly and get it in there as far as you can. Take me and make me all yours," Steve said.

"Okay, here I come. Get ready."

"Give it to me. I can't wait any longer to have you inside of me, baby," Steve said as Bulldog placed Steve's ankles on his broad, hairy, tattooed shoulders.

Steve remembered the feeling of having Bulldog enter him from the last time that they tried this and he braced himself for the shock of his entry. Bulldog lined up with Steve's hole and placed the tip of his latex covered cockhead against the opening of Steve's warm tunnel. He locked eyes with his lover and gave a gentle push to start his entry, but at the last second he gave a hard shove and his head slid inside easily. Steve started to heat up inside as Bulldog's cock led the way, pushing his entire pole into Steve's willing backside. Steve grunted with the combination of pleasure and surprise that was filling his body at that moment. He focused on his feelings for Bulldog and that made him feel that it was worth it for them to feel connected.

"I love you, Steve," Bulldog said as he started to slide his meat in and out of Steve's hole.

"I love you too. I want you to give me everything that you got big man!"

For the next 20 minutes, the two lovers journeyed though a land of passion that was beyond any that either of them had ever shared with anyone else. Bulldog stayed constantly focused so as to not let his emotions overtake him. Even at the moment of his release, he fought with every fiber of his being to keep his composure and for the first time in his life he had an orgasm that was fully enjoyed by his human side and not overtaken by the power of the wolf inside of him. The men climaxed together, Steve ejaculating thanks to the combination of Bulldog's cock inside of him and the big biker's hand working his stiff road with every stroke that he took in and out.

"That was incredible!" Steve said as he lay on the bed looking over at Bulldog, who was beside him, staring at him.

"You're so beautiful," Bulldog said and began to once again kiss him. A moment later Steve's hand reached down and gripped the stiffening cock of Bulldog.

"This genetic anomaly, can it be potentially passed through oral sex?" he asked.

"No, no it can't." Bulldog replied with a sly smile.

"Good. I want to practice that deep throating thing some more," he said as he slid down to take Bulldog's now fully hard again cock into his mouth. Bulldog lay back on the bed and closed his eyes. A smile moved across his face as he let the pleasure of what Steve was doing to him come over him. He felt he had learned for the first time ever to control his wolf instincts. He allowed himself to think that this may just work after all.

*****

Bulldog stood before his pack mates and biker brothers at the clubhouse. He was standing on the small round platform in the middle of the main room. The platform was normally in use by one of the many women who liked to hang around the club. They had installed a stripper pole on it to facilitate better entertainment for the guys. Tonight, however, it was Bulldog who was standing there addressing his club, for what he hoped would be the last time.

"Brothers. I have reached an impasse in my life that puts me at odds with the direction, mission, views and long-term goals of this club. I have, for a long time, been unhappy. Many of you know that. I have been looking for something to fill what I felt was a hole in my life. I have now found the thing that I felt that I was missing. I have fallen in love with someone, and it is someone that the leadership of this club does not agree with. I was told that I had to let go of the person that has brought me so much happiness in my life once more. I was told that I had to relinquish my happiness for the so-called betterment and good of this club. I am sorry, but I cannot do that. I have now been put into a position where I have been forced to choose between this club, this pack, this group of men who, for the past seven years, have been the only family that I have known and the person who I have given my heart to. For that reason, I have made the difficult choice to leave this club and pursue what is right for me. My staying will not benefit the club. It will only cause the continued distance between me and the rest of you to get bigger and thus create even more resentment and animosity. I cannot continue to wear the colors of this club with a true heart and, for that reason, I hereby resign my place among this brotherhood and leave this pack. I wish you all the best."

The silence in the room was deafening as the men stood there for a moment and tried to absorb what it was that they were hearing.

"So, what, you're giving us up, man? That's fucked up!" Mason finally said, breaking the uncomfortable silence.

"No. What's fucked up is the leadership of this club telling me that I had to either end it with the person that I have fallen in love with or they would see to it that this club ended it for me. We all know what that threat means and I won't have any part of a group that would treat someone like that, while at the same time calling them brother. As for this vest," he said, pulling it from his body and tossing it to Charlie, "you can take it. I'm done. I strongly suggest that this be the end of the matter for everyone as well. Don't come after me or try anything with me. I know how this club operates and I won't have it. This is my chance to be happy and if you guys love me as you say you do, then you will let me go." He could tell that the mood in the room was not supportive, but then again, he didn't expect it to be.

"There is one more thing," he said as he walked over to where Axel was standing. "You were my best friend. When I called you brother, I meant it more than I did with any other man in this room. But what kind of a buddy would deny his best friend, his brother, the one thing that he knew would make him happy? I know it was you…" Bulldog reared back and, as hard as could, he punched Axel square in the face and sent him reeling to the floor. He landed with a hard thud. The entire room was taken by surprise, no one more so than Axel himself.

"You are nothing to me now. Not friend, not brother, not pack. I don't want to know you, don't want to see you. When you come through town, until such time as I leave, make sure that you stay downwind from me because I don't even want to smell your stink, you sorry son-of-a-bitch!" Bulldog said. Axel started to try to stand, assisted by a couple of other club members standing on each side of him.

"You are writing a check your ass can't cash!" Axel said as he struggled slowly to get to his feet.

"Go ahead, asshole, stand up, so I can put you down again. All it will do is make me feel even better." The other two men stopped helping him and he dropped back to the floor. Axel looked up at him with a look of disdain. He knew damn well that in a fair fight, he simply couldn't take Bulldog. He also knew that this would not be a fair fight so he had no chance in hell that he would be able to come out on top. He just stayed down on the ground, looking up at the man who had just put him there and feeling like a cast away.

Bulldog looked around the room and, without another word, walked out of the building. A moment later the sound of his bike being started and pulling out of the lot could be heard.

"Boss, you cannot be serious about letting him walk away! No member of this club has ever hung up his vest and walked out," Damien said as he looked at Charlie.

"Don't worry boys. He won't be gone for long. I have a plan. He'll be coming back to us real soon. I promise you that." Charlie said with an evil squint in his eyes.

"How can you be so sure, Boss?" Gunner said.

"Simple. When a man has lost the thing that he cares about the most, he turns to family. We're his family, and he is about to experience a loss," Charlie said as he turned and walked away from the group to his office. It was time for him to take a drastic step to end this once and for all.

*****

# Volume Five – Transformation

Bulldog and Steve walked out of the theater after the movie had ended and started to walk down the sidewalk to where they had parked on the other side of the square. "That was an… interesting movie," Bulldog said.

"Be honest. It sucked!" Steve replied.

"Well, I didn't want to say anything, since you were so excited to see it but…"

"I know, I was wrong, okay? Next time you get to pick the movie," Steve said with a wink.

"That's probably the safest idea," Bulldog said as he put his arm around Steve's shoulder and pulled him closer as they walked. Steve put his arm around Bulldog's waist and then turned his head. Bulldog gave him a quick kiss. "I love you," Bulldog said.

"I love you too. I'm so glad that you're in my life," Steve said.

"Me too," Bulldog said in reply. "I wouldn't trade you for anything."

"Do you mean that? You gave up so much to be with me, after all," Steve asked.

"Yes, I do. I gave up a lot, but I got even more in return. More than I ever thought was possible to have," he said as they stopped.

Bulldog turned to Steve and looked deep into his eyes. He knew that things had reached the point in their relationship where he was soon going to have to deal with the secrets about himself and what he truly was that he had been trying to avoid for so long. He knew that he was going to have to make a commitment to Steve and, at the same time, he was going to have to tell him the truth about his other life. He had not yet figured out how to break it to him or even to begin to address everything that he would have to deal with, all of the questions that would inevitably come, but he knew that it was going to be soon. He owed Steve that much at least.

"So, what do you say about us heading back to my place and enjoying a little late night treat?" Steve asked as he ran his hands up and down Bulldog's heavy, flannel shirt.

"Oh! Choco-crazy fudge brownie ice cream with sliced almonds, chocolate sauce and mini-marshmallows?" The big man asked with a smile.

"Not quite what I had in mind, but we can start there," Steve said as he moved his hand down and started to gently squeeze the bulging crotch of Bulldog's very well-packed jeans.

"Oh, that. Well, I guess if you press the issue, I might be persuaded to cooperate, but only on one condition," he said.

"What's that?" Steve asked in response.

"That when I'm done pleasing you like you've never been pleased before, I can have..."

"Choco-crazy fudge brownie ice cream with sliced almonds, chocolate sauce and mini-marshmallows!" both men said in unison as they turned and started to walk once more hand in hand toward where Steve's car was parked.

As they turned the corner, Bulldog suddenly stopped in his tracks. Steve looked at him, wondering if everything was all right. Bulldog looked around wildly, a panicked expression on his face. He spun in all directions, his eyes scanning for what it was that had caught his senses. As he looked around, he knew what it was that he was picking up on but it seemed just out of his reach. He had never been all that good at tracking. It had always been a weakness of his. He had wished he had paid more attention when he was younger. His senses were going haywire nonetheless. He could smell them. He could hear them breathing in the dark. He could feel their presence. The bond of the pack still connected to his mind, his soul. The only thing he could not do was see them. He had no idea where they were, but he was sure that they were out there. He had been waiting for this. He had hoped that he had been wrong. He had wanted to be wrong about what he thought was coming, but deep down, he should have knowing better. He should have known that there was no way that they would ever let him go without trying to pull something.

"Babe, what's wrong?" Steve asked.

Bulldog looked at him and his eyes tightened. He was, for the first time in his life, genuinely scared. He had so much to lose now and he wasn't sure where to even start to protect the thing that he held so precious to him. 'Maybe this had been a bad idea after all', he thought to himself. It didn't matter now, though. It was what it was. He had made his decision and it was time to face the consequences. They were in it now. All he could do was try to get Steve out of there safely. He had made his own bed and now, if he had to lie in it, then so be it. He was damn sure that, before he went down, fighting every step of the way, he would take some of them with him. He would take all of them with him, if it meant that he ensured Steve's wellbeing and safety.

"Steve, run. Right now. Get to the car, get inside, and don't open the doors for anything, not even for me."

"What's wrong, Lucas?" Steve said. He was clearly shaken by the sudden change in Bulldog's behavior. He had never seen him in this way before. He had never seen the tough, biker side of him. He didn't know it but there was also another side of the big man that he had yet to see, one that was even more dominant and powerful then anything he could imagine. That was the side of him that was about to have to be used to defend them. To possibly even save their lives.

"Just do as I say, please. Whatever happens, know that I love you. Now, RUN!" he screamed, but it was too late. Out of the shadows of the alley came two large black wolves. Bulldog knew that it was too late at this point to do anything other than fight. That was the only option at this stage. He knew that he would have to stand against his former brothers to protect the man he loved. He also knew that his desire to keep his secrets was now a moot point. The secrets were about to be spilled and this was not the way that he wanted it to happen.

"Baby, what is going on?" Steve asked. Bulldog pulled Steve behind him and started to move him back to where his boyfriend would be between him and the brick wall to their rear.

"Stay behind me. Stay as close to me as you can. Don't move," Bulldog said.

"What is happening? Where are these dogs coming from? What's going on?" Steve asked.

"They aren't dogs. They are wolves," Bulldog said. From around the corner of the buildings, two more wolves appeared at the entrance of the alley. "Leave us alone. I told you not to bother us!" Bulldog screamed at the animals. Steve looked at them and wondered why he was talking to them like he knew them, as if they could understand what he was saying. Another two followed behind them and now blocked the entrance completely.

"Lucas...I'm scared. Please tell me what's happening!" Steve begged.

"It's a little complicated to go into right now," Bulldog said. "Why can't you guys just leave us be. Why do you have to be like this?"

Another wolf came from the shadows of the back corner and walked slowly toward them.

"I promised you that I would not tell and I haven't. He is not a threat to you, and neither am I," Bulldog said.

Finally, a very large wolf with bright red fur came out from the darkness of a doorway alcove and proceeded to jump onto the roof of Steve's car. The large red wolf looked right at Bulldog and snarled. Bulldog turned to face the red wolf.

"I said that I would not tell. I said that I would leave here and take him with me. Why can't you just accept that?" Bulldog said as he looked the wolf in the eye. Suddenly, to Steve's shock, the large red wolf started to morph into the shape of a very large man, right before his eyes. Soon, where the wolf had been standing on the roof of his car, now stood the impressively built, nude and very hairy-bodied leader of The Beasts Motorcycle Club.

"I told you that there was only one way that this would go, Bull. You chose for us to handle this instead of handling it yourself like a man!" Charlie said.

"I told you that I would not give up on the only thing that has ever brought me happiness in my life," Bulldog said.

"You cannot have that kind of happiness. You are one of us. You are a member of this club, a part of this pack!" Charlie said loudly. Steve was still in shock as to what he had just witnessed. He didn't understand what it was that he had seen. It was like some kind of weird dream.

"I am a man who has needs and desires, why can't you understand that?" Bulldog asked.

"You are a Werewolf! You have only the needs of your nature. To be free, to run, to eat and to breed!" Charlie said loudly. The words that had come out of his mouth echoed through Bulldog's mind the same as they echoed off of the walls of the alley. As he looked around, he suddenly saw the other wolves all change into naked men who now surrounded the two of them and were slowly moving in toward them with menacing looks on their faces and clenched fists.

"I don't want to fight you!" Bulldog screamed.

"Then don't. Just hand over sweet-cakes there and then take back your place in this pack," Charlie said.

"I won't let you kill him!" Bulldog screamed.

Suddenly the severity of the situation that they were in hit Steve. He was unable to fathom the reality of the fact that he was surrounded by a group of werewolves at the moment. That it was apparent that his boyfriend of the last three months was also one. That he had fallen in love with a creature that he had always believed to be a myth. All of that was spinning around his head as he tried to comprehend the fact that this knowledge may very well lead to his death now at the hands of these werewolves.

"We won't kill him, Bull. Hand him over and I promise he won't die. We can always use another club slave though!" The men all roared with laughter as they moved in closer still.

"No! He is mine!" Bulldog growled as he yanked his shirt off over his head and tossed it to the ground.

"Bull, don't make this harder than it has to be. He isn't worth it!" Charlie said.

"He is the only thing in my life that is worth it! You want him, you have to go through me!" Bulldog said as his voice deepened and became more guttural and animalistic. He turned to Steve and his eyes were a deep yellow color. "Run as soon as you can. Don't look back. Get home, lock the door and stay inside. I love you!"

A tear seemed to come out of his eyes as Steve nodded his head and let his fingers gently graze Bulldog's rock solid arm. The big man turned back to the pack of men, who were all in the same transition stage as he was. In a flash, it seemed they were all changed back into their wolf forms. Even Bulldog had fully changed, his body letting his clothes and boots fall away as he leapt forward and engaged the attackers. Steve saw his opening as the wolves started to fight a heated battle in the alley. He ran for the other side of the square, a wolf following him at full clip, until he jumped into the back of a parked cab, yelling "Get me out of here!" He looked back as the cab pulled away from the curb, the wolf stopping in mid stride just a second too late to catch its prey. Steve watched as the wolf glared at him, then turned and headed back to the alley to rejoin the fight.

*****

Steve sat at the counter in the kitchen, full of worry, and looked into his coffee cup. He was still in shock with what he had experienced but, more than that, he was scared. He was not sure how in the hell Bulldog could have survived the onslaught of the wolf attack that he was in the middle of. If he didn't survive it, Steve was not sure what he would do next. He was certain that they were going to come for him just as soon as they were finished with Bulldog. Suddenly, there was a knock at the back door, interrupting his thoughts. Steve jumped up and ran to the door. It was Bulldog, looking like he had just been through a war. Steve unlocked the door and the big biker ducked inside quickly, locking the door behind him and letting out a big sigh of exhaustion. He was naked, full of cuts and bruises. Steve assumed that meant he had come all the way here in his wolf form.

"Oh my God, I am so glad to see you!" Steve said as he put his arms around Bulldog's neck and started to hug him as tight as he could. He moved up and started to give the big man a deep passionate kiss, saying "How the hell did you get away from them?"

"Long story. Let's just say that there are two less wolves that are a threat to us now," Bulldog replied.

"I don't even want to know what that means," Steve said. He was pretty sure he knew what it meant but he was not sure how to accept that fact. "You're alive and okay, though. That's all that matters. How badly are you hurt?"

"I'll live, but I do need a first aid kit. Tell me that you have one, please," Bulldog said.

"Yeah, I have one upstairs. It's a huge thing, medical grade stuff. The ex was a first responder with the fire department. I bought it for him as a Christmas present. He never even opened it so when I left, I took it out of his truck and brought it with me," Steve said as he led Bulldog upstairs. As he tended to the wounds, he thought it was as good a time as any to address the 300-pound wolf in the room.

"So, let's take this from the start. Why didn't you tell me?" Steve asked matter-of-factly. Bulldog was shocked that the first thing that Steve asked wasn't the most obvious question. He wasn't sure how to react to that.

"I think that's rather obvious, isn't it? I mean, come on, your boyfriend tells you this kind of thing and the next thing you know I have a restraining order against me and you're calling the guys in the long white coats to come have a talk with me," Bulldog replied as Steve closed up his wounds with liquid suture and cleaned his scrapes and cuts with alcohol and peroxide.

"It doesn't matter. You say you love me and I know I love you and if we are going to spend the rest of our lives together then this is the kind of thing that I kind of need to know. I mean, I don't know how to handle all of this. Are you a man? A wolf? Do I have to get you shots or something? What the fuck do I do with this kind of information?" Steve said. Bulldog couldn't believe that he had just asked that. He found it cute and comforting that Steve was taking this seemingly so well. He was also in awe of what he had just heard.

"Do you mean that?" Bulldog asked.

"About the shots? Yeah, I mean that. I have no idea what the hell this all means. Do you need a license or what? How does this work?"

"No, not the shots part. Do you mean the part about spending the rest of our lives together?" Bulldog asked.

"Of course I mean it. I don't know why you kept this part of you from me. But it does not matter. I love you for you, the man I have grown to know. I assume that this does not change who he is?"

"Not one bit. And I love you as well, with all of my heart," Bulldog replied.

"So it's true though, right? I'm not crazy, you really are a..."

"Werewolf. Yes, I am. My father as well. My whole family, for many generations, going back to the old country in Europe. I am a natural born, but there are also turned wolves. It's caused by a virus that alters our genetics, changes our whole DNA code at the core. We are human, but we are also more than human and we can shift back and forth at will. That's why I had to wear protection when we had sex. It can pass to others, just like an STD. I didn't want to infect you as it's against one of our most basic laws. But falling in love with you is against our laws as well. We are not supposed to get intimately involved with regular humans. I wanted to make it work, somehow, but the truth is, I don't see how it can. They will never let me leave the pack. I see that now. They cannot allow me to ever be with a human in a relationship. It's just not something they can let happen. I'm sorry I got you into this," Bulldog said.

"I love you and I'm not letting you go that easy. I have waited my whole life for a man like you," Steve said.

"Me too."

"Then we have to do something. What if…what if I weren't human?" Steve asked.

"What do you mean? You don't mean…No! I won't do that. It's against the laws of my kind and, besides that, there is a risk, a very serious risk. Not everyone makes it through the change and my DNA, my form of the virus, is very strong because it is so old and long-running in my family line. There is a chance that you might die if I infect you," Bulldog said adamantly, standing up and walking around the room naked. Even as he was stating his objections, Steve looked between his large legs and saw the massive cock and huge balls that hung there holding the solution to their problem. He knew that what he was asking would mean a change to everything that he had ever known in his life, but if it meant being with Bulldog without restrictions or fear, then it was worth it.

"If I can't be with you, then I don't want to live anyway. As for the laws of yours, you seem to have gotten into enough trouble as it is, so I don't see where this is going to add any more fuel to the fire."

Bulldog thought about it and he knew that it was true. He also knew that there was only one way that they could be together. He knew that there was no way that the pack were ever going to let Steve be in peace, and that there was only one chance that they would leave him alone. Changing him was the only way he knew to save Steve's life at this point, even if that meant possibly ending it in the process.

"Okay. I will do this if you are sure that you want it, but I don't like it," Bulldog said.

"You don't have to like it. You only have to love me and agree to stand beside me if I need you in this," Steve said as he stood up and took Bulldog's hand in his own. He looked up into those beautiful gray eyes and smiled.

"Oh, you're gonna need me alright. More than you have ever needed anyone in your life. And I do love you," Bulldog replied as he leaned down and kissed Steve on the lips tenderly.

Steve reached down and slowly started to stroke Bulldog's massive hanging cock. The heft and heat of the big man's huge cock was still incredible to Steve, despite the fact that they had now been intimate numerous times. This was the first time that he was going to ever be able to enjoy Bulldog's full strength without having to have a layer of latex between them. Steve slowly lowered himself to his knees and started to lick the now stiffening cock of Bulldog, who just looked down at him with a look that expressed his mix of pleasure and trepidation. He had wanted to be with Steve without having to worry about what could happen since the first day that he had seen him. Now that the moment had actually arrived,   he felt both happy and scared. There was a chance that Steve might not survive the change. Even if he did, things would be very difficult for him for a long while.

At the moment though, as he felt the rough, wet surface of Steve's tongue work up and down along the top side of his now almost fully hardened cock shaft, he didn't care. The burning was starting inside of him and he was going to let it take him away. It was the fire of desire, the spark of breeding that every wolf felt when the time came to do what it was that they were genetically best at doing; spreading the virus that would propagate their continued existence. He looked down at Steve, working his mouth around the sheer immensity of his beer-bottle thick, 12-inches of rock hard man cock, and he gritted his teeth. He put his hand on the back of Steve's head and pushed hard, forcing his cock head past the other man's lips and sliding it deep into his throat in one long stroke.

"Take my hard cock. You're mine!" Bulldog said as he ground his throbbing head deep into Steve's mouth. Steve could not believe the sudden change that had taken place in Bulldog in what seemed like an instant. The big biker's hands were gripping the back of his head and were holding him in place as the hulking man's huge cock drove in and out of his mouth. He was now being full on face-fucked by Bulldog for the first time ever and he had to admit that he was enjoying it. He liked the fact that, for the first time, he was getting the full brunt of the raw masculine power that the biker stud had to offer. He gagged and choked on Bulldog's huge dick for more than five minutes while the big man fucked his throat, before pulling out and grabbing him under the arms.

With a heavy grunt and a lunge, he tossed Steve to the bed. He landed with a hard thump and in a split second, Bulldog was on top of him and holding him to the mattress. He looked up into the big man's eyes. They had changed to the yellow, shiny ones that he had seen in the alley. He also noticed that Bulldog's teeth were sharper and pointier looking and that his fingernails were longer and sharper as well. There was a low growling to his voice as he talked.

"You wanted this, little boy. You want to be a real man like me? You want my thick cock up your ass bare? My cum coating your insides? My swimmers invading you and giving you my gift, my curse, my life. You asked for it and now you're gonna get it!"

Steve knew that it was the other side of Bulldog that was talking. It was the wolf that was saying those things to him.

Bulldog flipped Steve over onto his belly and, with no further comment or delay, he felt the huge cock of the outlaw biker wolf drive deep into his rectum. The head piercing his anal ring and the entire shaft sliding inside of him, bare, dry and with only a single hard shove. Steve let out a primal scream as he was entered so pleasurably. He could feel his hole expanding, his insides being filled with Bulldog's thick, hard cock. His body had taken the massive organ of Bulldog many times but never like this. He had never been so tough, so in charge. Bulldog knew that, in order to convert Steve, he had to fuck him like never before, so that when he came inside of him, the virus would have a better path into Steve. His wolf side, that was currently in control, wanted to just drive harder, pound more aggressively and do as much as he could to make sure that his sperm found a home in the other man's body and gave up their precious cargo of Lichen DNA.

"Please..." Steve said as he struggled underneath Bulldog, who was now driving his long, thick cock in and out of his hole with a brutal stroke that made him feel like he was being ripped apart.

"Too late, little man. I'm going now. You're getting bred. No reason to beg me not to, it's gonna happen."

"No...Please! Please give it to me! Harder!" Steve said. Bulldog stopped for half a second and then smiled. He wasn't begging for him to stop. He was begging for him to do it, to give him the gift that he carried in his blood stream, the curse that he carried through his life.

"Hell yeah! Now you're talking!" Bulldog said as he began to fuck Steve even harder than before. He had a renewed fire inside of him that he had not felt in a long time. He was going to do it. The doubt, the fear, the regret were all gone. He was going to breed him. He was going to convert him. For the first time in his life, he was going to make someone else a wolf. He drove hard and deep inside of Steve's rectum and began to release his load of thick, creamy cum inside his lover's ass.

"Make sure it takes. Do whatever you have to do. Bite me if you have to!" Steve said as he felt the pulsing of Bulldog's massive member inside of him and knew that the load of thick, creamy cum that had been churned up by the big man's over-sized balls was now flooding his rectum with sperm that carried the DNA of the lichen virus.

As strong as the virus was in Bulldog's family line, he knew that just dumping a load of sperm inside of the other man was probably enough to get the job done, but he wanted to be sure that Steve converted. Bulldog knew that what Steve was asking would in fact make sure that the virus took hold. He bent down and bit hard on Steve's shoulder, opening up a series of small wounds from his sharp teeth. Next, he bit lightly at his own wrist and, when the blood started to trickle out, he pressed it to the bite wound on Steve's shoulder and smeared the entire area with his wolf virus infected blood. Both men smiled at each other as they realized that this was it; without a doubt, Steve was now infected and now it was just a matter of whether or not he would survive the transformation.

Bulldog slipped his huge cock out of Steve's ass and then lay down and held his lover tightly in his arms. Steve laid his head on Bulldog's hairy chest and moaned lightly with the pain that was filling his body from the bite and from the deep, rough, unprotected fuck he had just endured at the hands of Bulldog.

"So, now what happens?" Steve asked.

"Well, if the virus takes, then in a day or so you are going to get sicker than you have ever been in your life. Think about the worse flu you have ever had and then think of it being 20 times worse. It's going to last about a week or two and then, when your body has been ravished, when the virus has poisoned every cell, when you feel like you're only moments from death, then the change will happen. That's when you will be in the most danger. Even if you survive the sickness, your body may not be able to withstand the change," Bulldog said.

"Was it what way with you?" Steve asked.

"Yes. I got sick when I was 11. For males, it comes at the start of puberty. For females, it comes a bit later and is not nearly as bad. The virus seems to be affected by testosterone. The more you have, the worse it is," Bulldog said.

"I'm scared," Steve said. Bulldog moved closer to him and kissed his forehead.

"I know. I will be there for you the whole time. I will get you through it. You're strong. You will survive. I know you will," Bulldog said.

"I want to make sure it took. Fuck me again. Fuck me as many times as you can. Keep it hard and don't you dare waste a single drop of your cum, not a single sperm. Please."

Bulldog smiled and leaned in to kiss Steve passionately. "As you wish…"

****

"You have a lot of nerve coming here after what you did!" Mason shouted as he stood up and started to make his way toward Bulldog.

"I'm glad he came. It makes us killing him easier. We don't have to track him down!" Hutch said as he also started to approach Bulldog. He had a large knife out of the scabbard on the back of his belt. "I'm not even gonna change this time. Just gonna hold you down and cut your fucking balls off just like you did to Damien, you fucking shit! Gonna love to watch you bleed to death while I hold that monster dick and those over-sized baby makers in my fucking hand!"

"Parlay!" Bulldog screamed.

"Fuck that parlay shit. We're gonna rip you apart and eat you for breakfast for what you did to Damien and for killing Vince!"

The men in the room all started to move closer to Bulldog. He had a feeling that, considering the fact that he had in fact castrated one of the club brothers and killed another in the battle in the ally, not to mention wounding several others, some nearly fatally, that they would not honor the traditions of the biker world and grant him parlay but he had to try. He knew that if he had to, he would be able to fight his way out of there once more, but before it came to that, he wanted to at least make the attempt at peace. These men, this club, the pack, had been his only family for so long that he felt that he owed it to his own sense of honor to make good with them, even if that meant he had to face the consequences.

"Stop!" Charlie said as he walked into the room. He looked like the alley fight had taken a hard toll on his body. He was heavily bandaged and was still walking with a slight limp. He had taken the brunt of the battle on himself and it showed. Bulldog was also wounded significantly but he did not want to let the pack see that. That would only play into their hands. "He is a brother..." Charlie began to speak.

"He is a traitor and a killer of his own!" Mason interrupted, as he pointed the knife toward Bulldog. "According to our laws, for his treason, he forfeits his balls. For his killing of a member of this club, he forfeits his life. And I intend to claim them both. Damien is my best friend. Vince was my maker!"

"And they knew that Bull is a powerful wolf, as did we all when we decided to go against him. They paid the price for not being good enough in battle. But that is not the point to be argued at the moment. Right now, he is here on his own accord and has called for the right of parlay. Going back to the first outlaws, the pirates of the open seas more than 300 years ago, the right of parlay has been honored for all of those brothers who call for it. We will not disgrace our traditions more in this thing than we already have." Charlie said.

"But boss..." Axel exclaimed.

"But nothing. Silence! I am the alpha of this pack and the president of this club. Unless one of you wants to challenge that position right now, I have spoken. Parlay has been called for and is in effect. Bull, what do you have to say for yourself? You have put your life on the line, not to mention other things that you hold dear, to come here and say something today. What is it?" Charlie said as the men backed off, obviously upset by the choice of their leader, but still respecting his authority.

"What is done is done. I cannot bring Vince back. I cannot give back to Damien what he has now lost. But that was all done in self-defense, to protect myself and to protect Steve. I warned you all. If you had let me go like I asked, then this would not have happened. I am sorry for all that has occurred and I am willing to give myself over to the justice that our laws demand, but only on one condition. You agree to leave Steve alone, forever," Bulldog said.

"Why would we do that?" Mason said.

"Because our laws state that we cannot, unless it's under the cloud of war or in the protection of ourselves, cause harm to another wolf. Under no circumstances," Bulldog said.

"But he is not one....wait. No. My God, you didn't!" Axel said.

"I have," Bulldog said.

"Already? And you are sure he has changed?" Charlie asked.

"He has not changed, yet, but I fucked him hard and deep, multiple times in a row and came inside of him without protection. I also bit his shoulder and smeared my own blood into the wound. You all know how powerful I am and that I am a natural wolf from a very long heritage, one of the oldest family lines in Europe. He is infected, I can assure you of that. As such, it's only a matter of time, a very short amount of time, I might add, until he gets sick and then the change will come," Bulldog said.

"You're right, old friend. You are very powerful and your genetics are strong. For that reason alone, he may not survive the illness or the change that is about to overtake his body," Charlie said.

"If he doesn't, then so be it. He knew what the risk was when he let me breed him. He asked me to bite him to make sure the disease took. If he dies in the process, then you get what you want anyways. But if he survives it, and as strong as I know him to be, I believe he will, then the law is clear. Unless he causes you harm, he is not to be harmed," Bulldog said. "Agree to that and I will accept my punishment. I will allow you to castrate me for my treason, and I will allow you to take my life for my killing of Vince. I will not defend myself. I will let you do this to me because I deserve it."

For several moments the bikers in the room looked at each other and at Charlie and Bulldog standing before them. The two dominate men looked each other in the eyes without speaking. After a few minutes, Charlie finally broke the silence.

"You did what you did in self-defense. We attacked you and him. I am as much to blame for Damien's condition and the death of Vince as anyone. I damn sure am not giving up my balls or allowing anyone to slit my throat for the act. It's unfortunate but this needs to end here. Besides, what kind of a pack would we be to let a newly infected wolf go through the illness and first change alone? He is going to need a strong alpha wolf to get him through and to guide him as he learns to live his new life. To not allow him that guidance would be highly irresponsible. Almost as irresponsible as turning him to begin with, but that is neither here nor there," Charlie said as he walked toward Bulldog and then spoke to him softly, so that only he could hear. "Is this really what you want, Bull? Will this really make you happy?"

"Yes, it will" he replied.

"Okay then." Charlie turned and looked around at the other bikers in the room. "It is my judgment that, after careful consideration, the actions against this club to which Bulldog has been held are forgiven because of special circumstances. All, that is, save one. Bulldog, I find you guilty of the deliberate and willful infection of a human with our virus. For this act of grievous irresponsibility, I sentence you to ejection from this club and loss of all privileges and rights that membership affords you, complete banishment from this pack and I subsequently demand that you leave our territory within 30 days and never return here for the rest of your life unless summoned. I forbid you to ever join or attempt to form another pack or to wear the colors of another club for the rest of your life. You will, by your own hands, destroy your motorcycle at your first available opportunity that will not cause you undue hardship by leaving you with a lack of transportation to provide for yourself and those to whom you are responsible for the upkeep and well-being of. You will not ever purchase or acquire another one after that task is done and you will send to this club the VIN plate to show that this is finished. In that, I also sentence you to be responsible for the rest of your life to that which you have created. You will be held accountable for the well-being, the guidance, the training and all other aspects of the life of the wolf that you have made by breeding the human known as Steve, should he successfully survive the next few weeks of his life. Do you understand and acknowledge the conditions of this judgment? And do you understand that this judgment is final and is effective immediately?"

"I understand," Bulldog said as he stood in amazement at what he had just heard. He was going to get out of this alive and he was not sure how or why, but he knew that he wasn't going to question it.

"Then get out. You are not welcome here anymore. Make no mistake; we will be watching and if you do not comply, there will be no second chance, no more discussion, and no more mercy."

Bulldog looked around the room and saw that there was no desire for mercy in the eyes of his former brothers, even at this moment. He had no doubt that there would be none shown in the future as well. He also knew that they would never go against the wishes of their leader, or against his commands. More than that, he knew that if they ever did, he would be able to take them. He looked one more time around the clubhouse. He knew that he would never again stand inside the doors of the place that had been his home for so long. It was time to move on to the next chapter in his life. He turned and walked out the door. He felt good, he felt right.

*****

The afternoon was crisp and cool, like most afternoons in Southwest Montana in the summer. The sky was showing the signs of a light afternoon shower on the horizon, but the sun already starting to give way to the unexplainable beauty of twilight. Steve looked out at the lake. It was a view that he would never be able to get used to. So much had happened over the course of the last year. He had changed in so many ways, ways that he never thought were possible. He was happy though. He was happier than he ever imagined that he would be and it was all thanks to the man who had come into his life and sent it spiraling into a whirlwind of change. He didn't realize how much he needed that kind of Earth-shaking change in his life. Not only had Bulldog given him a new reason to live, he had given him a whole new life. He would never be able to thank him for that, but as he looked over at the other side of the deck, he knew that he would spend the rest of his life trying.

Bulldog sat on the other side of the deck and read the last few pages of the book that he had in his hand. His big cowboy boots were propped up onto the deck railing, His flannel shirt was open showing his white undershirt and his hairy chest underneath. His baseball cap was cocked back on his head. He closed the book and laid it on the side table beside him.

"So, how was it?" Steve asked.

"It's good. I have to admit, my Dad has an uncanny ability to make the violent overthrow of a pharaoh 2,500 years ago sound like a damn Agatha Christie murder mystery," Bulldog said as he picked up his beer and took a drink from it.

"I'm glad you're giving him the chance to build your relationship again. He wants to be a part of your life, babe," Steve said.

"Yes, and I owe that to you. I have to admit that when you approached him in the pizza place that afternoon and invited him to have lunch with us, I was not happy. Now, though, with us finally getting some of our problems worked out, that we have both carried for far too long, I am glad you did," Bulldog replied.

"I am happy I was able to help that happen," Steve said. "Almost as happy as I am to be here with you."

"Are you happy, really?"

"More than you know. I would not go back and change anything about my life since I met you. You are all I need to be happy, big man. The thing is, are you happy?" Steve asked.

Bulldog looked out at the lake. His motorcycle was sitting on the cement paddock near the entrance to the dock. He had not ridden it in over 3 months and that had just been once to town and back. He thought a few times of just rolling it down the dock and letting it sink to the bottom of the lake, a final farewell to the life that he had left behind. He knew that he wouldn't miss it, just as he didn't miss that life. There was a part of him though that still liked the thought of it being there, the idea that he might take it out every now and then when the nostalgia hit. If nothing else, it reminded him of how far he had come from that man he was so long ago. Truth was that he was happy. For the first time in his life, he was truly happy.

"Yes, I am happier than I have ever been before," Bulldog replied. Steve could see in his eyes that he meant it. Nothing else was needed to be said.

"Well, I don't know about you, but I know what I need for the perfect end to a perfect day, " Steve said as he stood up and started to strip off his clothes, leaving them in a pile at his feet on the deck.

"Ah, come on, babe. I mean, I love fucking you, but I can't go three times in one day. I'm not a machine. Now, a few years ago, I might be able to pull it off, but I ain't as young as I once was," Bulldog said with a smile as he watched his partner strip naked and stand before him. He was still in awe of how much Steve's body had changed over the last year. He was so much more muscular. His body hair, while abundant to begin with, was now thick and dark, and his manhood was larger than it had been when he had first met him.

"Very funny. But not what I had in mind, big man, at least, not at the moment," Steve said with a coy look on his face.

He suddenly jumped over the side rail of the deck. As he landed on the ground ,he did so on all fours, his wolf-form that of a large, powerful golden-haired wolf. Not only had the lichen virus taken a hold in Steve's bloodstream, but it had done so aggressively. The "flu" that he had endured was horrible; in fact, it had almost killed him. The first change had almost finished the job, but Bulldog had been there to nurse him and take care of him and bring him out of it. Now, he was as strong, as large and as powerful as the man who had infected him and turned him from human to lichen. Bulldog stood up and smiled.

"Now, that's not a bad idea! I could do with a good run myself," he said as he started to strip off his shirt and pulled his cowboy boots off of his feet and let them drop to the deck surface. He opened his well-packed jeans and pushed them to his feet before stepping out of them and pulling his white socks off. He stood before Steve wearing only his cap and his well-worn, well-packed jockstrap, heavy with the huge manhood that it kept under control during Bulldogs' day-to-day life.

"Tell you what. The large boulder on the other side of the lake is the finish line. First one there has to suck off the winner and do the dishes when we get back. Agreed?"

Wolf-Steve barked loudly in agreement as Bulldog pushed his jockstrap from his hips and kicked it off of his foot, high into the air, it landing on the ground beside the deck at the same time that he fully changed into his wolf form. The two wolves jumped at each other for a moment and then ran off to the entrance of the woods a few yards away, side by side, just like they would spend the rest of their lives, and happy to be doing so.

*The End*

\*\*\*\*\*

# Holiday Delight

Joanie - Joanna, really, but Joanie had been good enough for her mother and it was good enough for her - straightened out her skirt before she started to walk towards the printer. She had no time for the printer's antics. It sputtered and whirred, making an annoying high pitched noise before delivering a subpar product. She wished machines could be fired. Nevertheless, it was a necessary evil, one she used every single day. It had the decency to print all the files correctly for a change, Joanie thought, as she took the papers in her hands and straightened them out. She would take them home and read through them, snuggled up next to her designer pillows. She would wear her designer pajamas with her Gucci glasses and pace around, writing down notes on who needed to be called the next day.

"Joanie," her friend Michelle tapped her on the shoulder, "I think we have a meeting in the conference room in half an hour."

"Are you sure?" Joanie replied, staring longingly at the smart phone she had left on her desk. She wanted to check her schedule. She had checked it during the night, and was moderately sure that there had been no meeting announced.

Michelle nodded her head. "Yeah," she said, her big black hair bobbing up and down. Joanie blinked a few times. It was distracting. "Mr. Haverford just called it."

"Right, okay. When did you say?"

"Half an hour, woman! Pay attention." Michelle said, then

laughed.

Michelle was the only person in the whole company that talked to her like that. Of course, Joanie was the only one that got to call her Michelle. Everyone else got to call her Miss Swift. Michelle inspired fear in the hearts of many. It made her the perfect employee and a woman after Joanie's heart. They were truly equals in the workplace, and if Joanie had a best friend, it had to be Michelle. Not that she had much time for friends, but neither did Michelle, so that suited her just fine. The dark haired woman approached her and started to whisper into her ear.

"You know, I had difficulty taking the new boss seriously, but damn, is he fine."

"Ugh," Joanie rolled her eyes, "As far as I'm concerned, either one of us would be better suited for that gigantic office. Giving it to his forty year old son is just cronyism at its best, Shell."

"Hot cronyism, though," Michelle said, wiggling her eyebrows up and down.

Joanie smiled despite herself, pushing her friend playfully and biting down on her lip. Her voice was barely a whisper when she spoke again.

"You can't say that. He's our boss."

"Well," Michelle straightened up, "Hopefully not for long."

She winked and walked back to her office.

Joanie cracked her neck as she watched her walk away. What did Mr. Haverford have in mind? She wished she had asked Michelle if it was only the senior workers who had been called into the room.

She shrugged it off, realizing that she didn't have that much time to think about it, and continued to walk towards her office. There was so much she had to do, she couldn't even believe she had been called into a meeting that would cut into her day.

"Calm down," she told herself. Listening to her own voice was reassuring. "It's just a meeting."

It wasn't just a meeting. It had started at just a meeting, of course. The conference room had been packed. The firm employed around fifty people, and they were all there. She could see the janitor and the person who took care of the mail among the attendees. A little late, she squeezed past a few warm bodies. Michelle waved at her from a seat. If only she had finished that conference call earlier. She tried to smile at Michelle, but it turned into a grimace. She knew that even the places they chose in the conference room could determine their futures in the company.

Mr. Haverford was saying something. Joanie looked at him. He was a handsome man, with a full head of black hair that he carefully tamed every morning, small glasses that emphasized his tall cheekbones and curious brown eyes. His face was framed by arched eyebrows. There were crow's lines around his eyes from laughter and an easy demeanor, and his smile seemed to be permanently painted on. He was a little bit overweight, maybe around ten pounds, but his broad back and muscular arms made it so that the weight was evenly distributed on his body. Joanie shook her head, trying to get the less than savory thoughts out of her head. She tried to concentrate on what he was saying, watching his mouth move as he spoke. Damn, his lips were so sexy...

He smiled as he continued with what he was saying.

"So, what all those numbers mean is that our company has done extremely well over the past year. That is a credit to everyone that works here. From Mr. McIntyre, our janitor, to Mrs. Gomez, our head of sales," he pointed to these people as he said their names, "We are an incredibly well organized little machine, and we have all done our part. Without any one of us, we would not have been so successful. Now, success does carry on to financial success - and that means that this year, I will be getting a big check on top of my yearly salary."

People weren't muttering yet, but they had started to look at each other, questioningly.

"Some of you are in positions that don't get holiday bonuses. Well, these holidays, I want to thank you all personally. I will divide my bonus and give it to you, or well, what my accountant allows."

Everyone laughed, including Joanie. Mr. Haverford waited for the laughter to quiet down, and cracked a smile before continuing. He waved his arm around in a gesture before he spoke.

"So, I think we can gather from what I have just said that, that we have all been working extremely hard lately. Without all of your contribution, our company would not be doing nearly as well." He paused for a second, clearing his throat before he spoke again.

"We are not retail, guys. We do not need to be here for the holidays. Everyone of you needs to catch up on your sleep and with your family. What we do here - well, it can wait. I'm giving everyone two weeks off, paid. You should tie up whatever you are working on now," He looked straight at Joanie. His eyes burned through her, "And not worry about it for the time you have off. Enjoy your holidays, do some shopping or whatever. Be happy! Okay, you all have stuff to do, so you are dismissed."

Joanie made a beeline to her desk. Her head was spinning. Should she have volunteered to work for longer? Maybe that would have shown how committed and ambitious she was. She reproached herself as she sat down on her comfortable chair, wondering if her boss was going to pass her up for a promotion because of how things had gone down in there. She thought about that as she organized the files on her desk, thumbing through them to see if she could find any numbers she needed to call before the weekend.

Michelle appeared next to her, smiling. "I'm looking forward to spending more time with my son," she told Joanie.

Joanie smiled at her. She did want a break, but it wasn't like she had any children or family to look forward to. Nevertheless, she thought as she dialed the client's number on the office phone, maybe she did need it after all.

The first day off was wonderful. Joanie slept in, waking up only when rays of sunshine made their way into her room through her blinds. She yawned and turned her television on, watching the morning news. She went out for a coffee, had a salad for lunch, finished reading a book she had kind of been reading for a long time, watched a few movies and talked to her mother on the phone. She had a glass of wine at night before she went to bed. Sunday was more of the same, and she only got out of her pajamas when she had a nice long bubble bath.

By Monday, Joanie was struggling to find things to do. She cleaned her windows and the gutter, trimmed the trees in her yard and thought about repainting her mailbox. She picked up the phone to call Michelle, who said she was actually in Disney World, and they would have to talk later. She went through her address book trying to find other friends to socialize with only to come to the horrible, crashing realization that all the people she knew were clients. Her family, most of whom she was close to, lived thousands and thousands of miles away, and although she was happy to speak to them, it wasn't like they didn't have lives themselves. They were surprised and glad to hear from her, but after ten minutes of conversation, neither party had anything left to say.

She paced around her house wondering what to do, watching movies on repeat and talking herself out of going to the office. How was she supposed to survive two entire weeks of that torture? It wasn't like she could just travel. She already had travel plans for her scheduled vacation in February. She never traveled around Christmas time, the holidays annoyed her enough without having to go to an airport and listen to whiny crying children being transported from one end of the country to the other.

By Wednesday, Joanie was going crazy. What was she supposed to do? And why had she thought it was a good idea to buy such a big house in the first place? The rooms were empty and she was fairly sure that getting a guest bedroom when you never had any guests had been stupid. Joanie paced the halls of a house that was way too big for her, that she didn't really spend that much time in and tried not to cry. The realization that she wasn't just a good worker, but someone who spent her time burying herself in work because she had nothing else to do made her feel sick to her stomach.

What if she never did go up in ranks? What if Haverford never did promote her? Technically, Michelle had more to gain. She had a little kid to take care of. Joanie had nothing to take care of but herself. She thought about buying a pet, but she wasn't sure if she could put enough time and effort into it to really make it worth it. She couldn't sleep at all that night. The next morning she got up, made herself a latte and drove the to the office. She was going stir crazy, and she wanted to have something to take her mind off things.

She parked in front of the building. It was one of the bigger ones downtown, towering over all the other grey ones that marked the skyline. She pressed her identification card against the magnet strip in the garage. She drove into the parking lot, slowing down as she arrived at the parking spot specifically reserved for her. Joanie stepped outside of her car, dressed in a long pencil skirt and a loose white blouse, her outfit covered by a long blue coat and her hair up in a messy bun. She put the keys in the lock and pressed the heavy metal door to enter the building, licking her lower lip as she did so. Normally, the office was full, noises filling up the room as people spoke about their days and any other business. Today, she could hear nothing but the wind whistling outside, rattling the tiles on the roof.

She made a beeline for her desk, trying to concentrate on anything other than the lack of noise. She hated that she was the only person that had been desperate enough to come back to the office. Joanie wheeled her chair away from her desk and sat down, kicking her shoes off and booting up her computer. There was something to be said for having the massive building all to herself. It wasn't like she could literally put her feet up when her employees were around her.

Normally, she wore a bluetooth piece and listened to music from her computer when she wasn't on the phone, but not today. She plugged her speakers in and cranked the volume up, deciding to indulge in her guilty pleasure of 70s disco. "Boney M was the best band," She told herself as she started to check her e-mails. She wouldn't have admitted it to herself, but being in the office had centered her, made her feel instantly better. She felt like she belonged, like she could do something. She scanned through the e-mails that have been sent and started writing the priority ones that she needed to reply to in the legal yellow pad that she kept in her drawer, neatly placed against her collection of pens, staplers and erasers.

She was absorbed in her work when she heard someone clear their throat behind her. She put her feet down and made her chair swing back violently, the feeling that she had been caught doing something terrible making her heart beat so fast it felt like it was going to jump out of her chest. She took a deep breath before she opened her eyes, ready to confront whoever had cleared their throat and asked them if they had permission to be there.

As she did so, however, she saw Mr. Haverford, a befuddled smile on his face. She blushed and straightened her skirt, hiding her bare feet behind the wheels of the chair. Her attempt to be sneaky failed spectacularly, as she only managed to lose her balance and stumble forward, the chair landing squarely on top of her. Mortified and with her mouth against the greyish blue carpet, she put her arms in front of her and picked herself up.

"Eh, um, sorry," she mumbled, way too quietly for him to hear.

He was still standing in front of her, biting his lips and obviously holding back laughter. His hand was extended towards her. She took his hand and picked herself up, looking down, trying not to look at him.

"So, uh, thanks."

The smile in his voice was plain to see, "Yeah, you're welcome."

"Sorry, I..." Joanie replied, looking around her workspace, "I didn't think there would be anyone here."

He laughed, throwing his head back. It wasn't an ill-intentioned laugh. It was the laughter of someone who had heard something genuinely funny. When he looked at her again, his eyes sparkled.

"Yeah, me either, to be honest."

"Sorry," she mumbled, unable to look at him for too long and grimaced, "Do you think we can just forget about this?"

"Sure," He said, shrugging, "How about we go for a cup of

coffee instead? We'll have the kitchen all to ourselves."

She caught herself nodding despite herself. Why did she revert to a teenager when he was around? She was trying to impress him, not seem like a flighty schoolgirl, she reminded herself as she followed him into the kitchen. It looked like a different place without people in it. It was a little nook with an expensive coffee maker and a newer model microwave, a couple of tables with chairs and a spiral staircase that led to the canteen/cafeteria. It had recently been renovated, and it was easily Joanie's favorite part of the office. She was still wearing no shoes as she sat down and waited for him to put the coffee in. Mr. Haverford was whistling the song she had been listening to.

"You like Boney M?" she asked.

"Guilty," he replied, "They are groovy. To be honest, and you can't tell anyone this, I was in a disco cover band in college."

She burst out laughing.

"Really?"

"Yeah," he said, "You may not believe it 'cause you always see me in a suit, but I used to be quite the groovy guy."

"Groovy?" she raised her eyebrows.

"Whatever the term is for cool these days," He replied, pressing the button to start making the coffee. "I'm not that old but college feels like a lifetime ago."

"Yeah, tell me about it," Joanie replied, rubbing her feet together. There was a moment of silence in which she looked out the window. "Listen, I'm sorry if I interrupted you. To be honest, I was going a little stir crazy at home."

He nodded, sitting across from her. He was wearing a button up dark gray shirt and smart looking black jeans.

"Yeah, I know how you feel. I have about a million things to do and, well... I didn't want to do them alone."

"Oh?" Joanie could have sworn that Mr. Haverford had a long-term partner. He had brought her to functions and parties. He must have seen what she was asking about because he shook his head and waved her away.

"We broke up," he said, "She didn't want a commitment and I did. Turns out I'm an old fashioned type. To be honest, Joanie, I'm not getting any younger. We spoke about marriage a couple of times and she made it very clear that it wasn't just not on her list of things she wanted to be, but she also didn't want a lifelong commitment. I don't think I would have minded not being married, but certainly knowing she thought I was tradable..."

He looked up at her, looked down, blushed and cleared his throat.

"Sorry, don't mean to dump it all    on you. My house is just way too big without her. Anyway, what about you?"

"No drastic life changes, just a family that lives far away and the realization that I spend so much time at work it turns out I don't really have any friends," Joanie replied bluntly.

"Well, I guess we're both here for good reason, then" he said, getting up and pouring the coffee into the styrofoam cups. "How do you take your coffee?"

"Black, two sugars," she said. She had never been served coffee by the boss, and it turned out that she liked it quite a bit. She smiled widely at him, her teeth showing a little spot of lipstick that she had accidentally smeared on their whiteness. He placed the cup of coffee in front of her and sat down across from her again, a smile still painted on his face.

"I have to admit, you look very nice for someone just randomly deciding to come into the office," he said after a few moments of silence.

Joanie could have sworn she saw him blush. She looked straight at him, her eyes sparkling.

"Thank you, Mr. Haverford. To be honest, I have been very disheveled lately, just staying at home. It felt nice to just, you know, dress up."

"Yeah, I bet," he replied, "I feel a little stupid with what I'm wearing." He took a sip of his coffee. "You know, I wish you wouldn't call me that. My name is Anthony."

"Well, okay, Anthony." She wanted to ask if she could call him Anthony every time they interacted, including when there were other employees around. He seemed to read her mind, chuckling a bit before he waved at her, speaking.

"My father was Mr. Haverford," her boss replied, "Well, I guess he is, but he is retired now, so everyone calls him John."

"John?" She raised her eyebrows. She had never known her former boss's full name.

"John Anthony Haverford, the second," he laughed. "I'm the

third, but John is such a boring name, I started going by Anthony in college. Not that it is much cooler..."

"Are you kidding? Joanie is a stupid, stupid name," she replied, despite herself.

She found that he was easy to talk to, and that he had given her way more of the company she was craving than she felt like she deserved. After bantering with each other for a while, their coffee cups long empty, the woman looked at the circular clock hanging on the popcorn wall. They had been talking for nearly two hours. He followed her eyes, reading the clock and looking puzzled.

"Wow, we have been talking for a while."

"Yeah," she bit her lower lip, suddenly terribly afraid that she had been taking too much of his time, "I guess."

"No, don't worry, I didn't mean it like that. I have to admit that this is the most fun I have had for a while. You're a very interesting woman, Joanie."

"Thank you, Mr... Anthony." She could smell his cologne. He smelled so good, she could hardly contain herself. What was she feeling? It was like she had drank a bottle of vodka much too quickly.

"Are you okay?"

"Yeah, I think... I have high blood pressure or something," she smiled apologetically, wanting to laugh at her own private little joke.

When was the last time a man had excited her that much? He walked over to her and put a hand on her shoulder, moving in close to her and whispering something in her ear. She felt the hair on the back of her neck stand up as she felt his slow breathing, his aftershave so close to her she could smell it without moving an inch. She felt her heart beating in her ears. She wanted to turn around and kiss him, right then, put her lips over his and fall into his arms. She told herself to behave, her feet moving around as she struggled to keep herself under control.

He leaned in even closer and spoke in her ear, "I think I have high blood pressure myself."

"You do?" She turned around to look at him.

He put his hands on her shoulders and kissed her, his lips warm and soft against hers. She opened her eyes, shocked, then closed them and gave in to the sensation spreading all over her body, trying not to think about where she should put her arms. After the kiss was over, he moved back, looking rather shocked himself.

"Sorry, I'm not sure... I'm not sure what I was thinking."

"It's okay," she replied.

And it was okay. She had enjoyed the kiss; she just wasn't prepared to face any complications that may arise. Considering complications was already rather premature, since it had just been a kiss, but it had lasted a while, and he was still very close to her, to the point where she could see the tiny lines on his lips and the wrinkles around his eyes that he got from laughing all the time.

Before she knew what she was doing, she was leaning forward and kissing him back, her arms around his neck. She was shorter than him and holding herself up as she kissed him deeply. She could feel herself getting warmer and warmer as the kiss went on for a while. She broke away from him and stared at him for a second, her hand on the top of his buttons and ready to rip his shirt off. He looked at her curiously, a half-smile on his face.

"Are you okay?"

"Yeah, I'm just..."

There were so many thoughts going through her mind. She wanted to ask him if being with him would complicate or hinder her career, she wanted to ask him if he took her seriously and she wanted to know how much he wanted her, all at once.

"Taking the situation in."

It was an oversimplification, but it wasn't a lie, she thought. He pulled her close to him, the smile still on his face.

When he spoke, his tone was reassuring, and his voice was soft. She felt like putty in his arms.

"Look, I don't know where this is leading, either. I promise I'll give you a good day, and then we can see what happens. I have wanted you since the first moment I saw you..."

Joanie smiled, letting go again. She kissed him again, this time slowly undoing his buttons, her fingers burning as she finally got to touch his chest, tracing the outline of his pectoral muscles with her fingertips and touching him softly until she got to his trousers. It had been so long since she had undone someone's buttons that she fumbled until he decided to help her with his right hand, his left hand placed squarely on the back of her neck.

She grabbed his trousers' waistband and dropped them to the floor. She could feel the bulge in his Calvin Klein briefs, visible under the elastic blue fabric. She didn't dare glance yet, but she could tell from touch that he was a well-endowed man. She felt herself getting even more excited, becoming more eager as she finally took a peek down. She took a breath and moved away from him for a second.

"Sorry... it's been so long for me."

"That's okay," he said.

He grabbed her by her buttocks and guided her so that she could put her legs around his waist. Before she knew it, she was being carried by him. They arrived at his office, at the other end of the floor, giggling between kisses before he closed the door behind him and laid her softly on the oak wood desk. She undid a couple of the buttons at the top of her blouse, revealing a pale pink bra, her hands sweaty from how she felt. Before she could process what was happening, he had lifted up her blouse and was kissing her stomach, his tongue swirling around in circles until he finally reached her neck. He was almost entirely on top of her. She moved her skirt upwards, ready for him, a wet spot already spreading in her panties. She was biting her lips, tiny beads of sweat forming on her forehead. He moved his fingers downwards and started to touch her over her sink green panties, moving his long fingers over her slit. He moved her panties to the side and teased her, slowly putting a digit inside of her, only a little bit, until she was whimpering and asking for more. He obliged, putting his finger deep inside of her, faster and faster, until her toes were curling and she was begging him to be inside of her. He smiled at her coyly. "Okay, since you ask so nicely."

He climbed on top of her again and with her help, guided himself inside of her. She felt pleasure spreading from her groin all the way up her spine, the fact that she was incredibly excited plain to see in the way that he had easily done so. She grabbed his shoulders as he started thrusting into her, deeper and deeper, very close to her. She closed her eyes and enjoyed his scent and the way he felt inside her until she couldn't take it anymore. "Harder!" She demanded.

He did as he was told, going harder and faster, feeling himself get closer and closer to orgasm as she whimpered more and more. She clung to him as her toes curled and the sensation spread all over her body, the orgasm causing her extremities to go numb, even her lips, which were in an O-shape as she felt pleasure, tingled.

A few minutes later, after they had cleaned themselves up, Joanie still lying on the desk and trying to recover from what had just happened, her breathing still shallow, looked up at him. He had brought her a huge glass of water. She took it and drank it greedily, barely looking at him or offering him any. He smiled at her once she had finished. "Are you okay?"

She wiped her mouth with the back of her hand, completely forgetting her manners. "Yes, I am fine. Thank you. And you?"

"I'm good, I had a lot of fun."

A million questions flooded Joanie's brain. Had she ruined her career? What was she thinking? She wanted to get up and pace around, but her limbs were still barely responding to her commands. "Yeah, I had a lot of fun, too."

"Listen, Joanie," He sat down on his massive leather chair,

behind the desk. He was stroking her hair, "I don't want you to think that this is going to have an impact on your career."

"You read my mind," She replied, "I was a little worried about what was going to happen."

"You are very ambitious, and great at your job. If you think I haven't noticed you, you are very much wrong," He continued. "I haven't been completely honest with you, Joanie."

Her ears perked up instantly. Had she just sacrificed her future for a bit of lust? What had she done?

He laughed, waving her away. "Don't look so worried," He said, the laughter still in his voice, "It's nothing bad. I am, well, my father, has left me a lot of money. Like, a lot more than this company makes. Haverford is my grandmother's maiden name, my father's real name is Gregorio."

She swallowed. "Your father is John Anthony Gregorio? The mogul that owns half of the world's telecommunication systems?"

"Yes, and I have a lot of money and time. To be honest, I wanted to try my hand at being a CEO before I went on to travel the world with my ex and do everything else I wanted. I wanted to know what it felt like to be - to feel responsible," He continued. He sounded like he was talking more to himself than he was to her. "Anyway, I've been looking for a PA, someone that would have to travel with me... The work would be hard but a lot of fun, it would have to be someone I like, and they would be very handsomely rewarded."

Joanie looked at him. He went on. "Please don't misunderstand.

I would love it if you wanted to be with me, but you don't need to-"

She leaned over and planted a long, warm kiss on his lips. His eyes sparkled when she pulled away.

The night held never-ending promise.

*****

# Hunting Desire

Day broke only slightly in the short hours of late fall. After an unbearably dry summer, cooler air seemed to give crispness to the cedar trees along the highway. The low rumble of a pickup as it shifted gears uphill rang through the fog.

'*Big city hunters,*' Toriana thought.

It was, after all, that time of year. They would descend upon the county, one shiny four wheel drive at a time, and do what they could to blend in to a life they both envied and found laughable. There was novelty in test-driving the lifestyles of the locals, only to abandon it for their concrete jungle on Sunday evening. They, their suspiciously clean ATVs in tow, would exit via the main highway, leaving their kills behind for processing. Toriana only hoped she would not have a parking lot full of customers at the shop when she arrived. She was doing all she could to keep up with fall's onslaught. She winced a bit as she rounded the sweeping curve just before her turnoff. She would soon have the taxidermy shop and wild game processing house where she spent her days in view.

"Good, I beat them in." she sighed to herself as she turned into the parking lot.

Wittlich Taxidermy and Processing had been a staple in the community for well over 50 years. Toriana's great grandfather, a second-generation German immigrant, opened the business in hopes of marrying his lifestyle to his work. The concept was born of necessity and had managed to serve its purpose while simultaneously serving the community's needs. It was a win-win and had enabled Toriana's family to not only survive but also thrive in a world that could turn on them in an instant.

Toriana's great grandfather was well aware of the tragedy that could befall his family at any moment. His father and grandfather fled Germany to avoid just such persecution. They vividly remembered seeing their kind sought out for extermination. Visions of flesh being torn from screaming bodies plagued them and the smell of their burning brethren was never far from their waking thoughts or sleeping nightmares.

The werewolf was the hunted in those days and many fled the German countryside. Upon immigrating to the United States, the Menken family became Wittlich and began a life of relative anonymity. Blair County's sprawling hillsides and abundant wildlife made it a haven for werewolves. Soon, pack after pack found it's way into the area. After the Wittlich pack came Fahrenholz, then Krams-Klein, then Bedburg. What looked to be a thriving community of German immigrants was, in fact, a network of werewolf alliances and power structures.

The hunting areas were divided and deals were struck among pack leaders to ensure "fairness" among the packs. It was a paper utopia. There was no persecution and no civil war but not for lack of disagreement. The elders, in those days, kept their packs in check by reminding them of the old ways in the motherland. They feared that battles among the packs would expose them to the surrounding populous and, once again, lead to mass torture and murder of their kind. With charred bodies now a distant memory, alliances were strained and modern diplomatic manipulation became the law of the land. The shop had managed to keep the Wittlich pack at the top of the heap.

Toriana's senses peaked as she turned the key in the lock. There was something stirring inside. Perhaps it was her nature or perhaps it was the countless hours she spent on her grandfather's knee that fueled her hyper vigilance. Nonetheless, she steeled herself for battle as the door slid open with an unwelcome whine.

Toriana was a lithe woman of twenty-eight. Agile and athletic, she possessed a tenacity that belied her small stature. Even in human form, years of backbreaking work, coupled with a distaste for dependence, had made her a formidable opponent. Now, as she began to shift form in preparation for what might lay in wait behind the door, her eyes glazed and pupils collapsed to detect the faintest movement in the darkness. A ripple of muscle coursed down her back and through her shoulders and arms and her now elongated teeth pressed into her lower lip.

She smelled blood beyond the crack in the door and threw it open, nearly taking it from it's hinges. There, directly in front of her, the beast stood. Pieces of the animal in its grasp were strewn about the room. The concrete floor was awash with blood. Toriana stood and, in her rage shouted, "What the hell, Evan?"

Hearing its name, the beast began to shrink. Long limbs shortened and coarse fur seemed to retreat into flesh that became more supple as it drew together. The claws that had just a breath ago been tearing at flesh were reduced to surprisingly well-groomed nails. Evan was now precariously crouched on the floor, naked, and almost looking embarrassed for his position. Toriana knew that questioning him at this point would be futile. Evan would be too disoriented from his kill and she would be too angry to make much more sense than he would.

Toriana closed her eyes and breathed deeply. This was a method she learned over the years so that she could prevent a full shift. She was thankful for the progress her kind had made. Toriana was a different breed of werewolf than those of ancient horror stories. The elders called them Mischling or "the half blood". The occasional mating of werewolf and human throughout her bloodline had given Mischlings more control over their blood lust and the ability to shift at will.

However, there was a catch. Immortality was a characteristic no longer possessed by what she called "domesticated" werewolves. As a perk of this lost power, Toriana and generations before her had been given the opportunity to grow and age just like the humans around them. It made them less obvious. She looked at it as a survival mechanism. Toriana found that control, however, was all too often a question of free will.

As evidence to this phenomenon, there stood Evan. Typically a cheerful and bright young man, Evan's carnal pull ran deep. He, like many of the young men in the Blair county hoard, was known to seek out the thrill of the kill. Toriana looked down upon this behavior. She saw these young men in the same light as binge drinking frat boys who terrorized the college town a few miles up the highway. Seeing Evan in his blood drunk stupor was all the more troubling. Although, under cleaner circumstances, she would not have argued with the image currently in her sight.

Evan shook off the muscle stiffness of his shift and rose to his full stature. He was a solidly formed man whose medium height extenuated his muscular frame. As he stretched his arms backward, the two solid blocks of muscle covering his chest separated to reveal a guideline toward the v-shaped indentations in his lower abs. Toriana's eyes followed the flow of his skin downward, catching herself and stopping short of the feature presentation. Her eyes shot up to meet his.

She caught up with her breath and warned, "You will clean this madness up, now!" She passed him, as closely as she could without giving herself away. Quite predictably, he reached out and took her arm into his grip.

He pulled her ear to his face and whispered, "Yes I will. I didn't know that you would be here so early so you don't have to play hard ass with me. I know better, remember?"

She pulled away and went to back of the shop. Losing strength in her legs, she leaned against the wall to steady herself. She did remember. She remembered the summer before when he made her powerless for the first time. She remembered moaning in his arms with reckless abandon and giving in to him entirely. Even now, standing alone, she felt a spreading heat. Her hands involuntarily began to trace his path. Her sigh of phantom release, even though soft, shocked her out of her fantasy. She knew she must make a display of dominance now or risk having him think she would abide his behavior indefinitely.

Toriana stormed back into the main area of the shop and threw at Evan a soiled pair of coveralls. Not risking giving him the opportunity to speak, she verbally attacked.

"This is bullshit, Evan. I really don't care what happened between us or how long you've worked for my family. I'm done with these little boy antics. You are a grown man and it's about time you get your head and your ass wired together. Now put some damn clothes on and deal with this disaster because I'm not going to anymore."

She crossed her arms in a mock invitation for rebuttal, but received none. She turned and walked away, thankful for avoiding an argument.

Satisfied that the bustle outside was Evan cleaning, Toriana settled into her desk. She heard a chime from her computer and opened her email. At the bottom of a long list of subject's lines, one caught her attention. *Reminder: Council meeting tomorrow 6 pm.*

The council met only twice a year, making each meeting long and busy. She hated council but knew that her presence was necessary to ensure her seat on the council once her father retired. He all but had retired already. Toriana wasn't sure if he was holding on to his seat because he couldn't admit to himself that it was time to let go or because of the councils fevered opposition to his passing the torch to a daughter. She openly resented the boys-club nature of hoard affairs and had spent the better part of her life resisting it.

Having no siblings, Toriana was the only option for filling her father's seat while maintaining bloodlines. The Wittlichs had maintained good relationships with other packs within the hoard. The shop employed several young men from various packs and the very nature of the shop served as a mechanism to cover up the occasional indiscretion. Dietrich Wittlich, Toriana's father, was quite the politician. During his time on the council, he had managed to negotiate a better balance of hunting grounds between the Bedburg and Fahrenholz packs and had even quelled a near civil war when the Krams-Kleine pack split into separate factions.

Even with the business at hand, Toriana could not fully turn her attention away from Evan's presence in the next room. She toyed with the idea of apologizing. She had no real remorse for anything she had done but, instead, saw it as an excuse to strike up conversation. Toriana seldom felt remorse. Emotional attachment was a crutch in her mind. Just as the werewolves who hunted for the kill alone and not out of any necessity, Toriana sought out the company of men for sport.

Then there was Evan. She was not altogether sure for what reason Evan occupied her mind. The only thing that she knew for certain was that he did. She resented him for it. How dare he assume to invade her thoughts? The anger and outrage at his ability to skew her perception fueled deeply burning passion. She felt a need to seek him out, a drive which only exaggerated the problem. It was tiring.

Before realizing it, she was again in the front room of the shop. It was empty. The gore and its creator were little more than a memory. The stillness was interrupted by the ringing of the phone.

"Wittlich taxidermy and processing, this is Toriana." she said in robotic monotone. Dietrich's welcome voice hummed through the line.

"Good morning, baby girl" he paused "you sound thrilled. What's wrong?"

Trying to maintain her bearing she replied, "Daddy, you have got to do something with Evan. I walked in this morning and it looked like he'd tried to paint the place with deer blood. It is out of control."

Dietrich chuckled, "Boys will be boys, my dear. You shouldn't be so hard on him. After all, he's only doing what comes naturally. Did he at least clean it up?"

Feeling more than a little patronized, Toriana hissed, "After I chewed his ass he did."

Dietrich, seeing no harm in the situation, quickly changed the subject.

"Well, I need you at the council meeting tomorrow. There are some important matters that need to be addressed. That Krams-Kleine business has heated up again and I do not think that I can cool it without your help. Will you be there?" he asked.

Toriana was pleased but unsure of her father's meaning. Without asking for further explanation, she assured him that she would be by his side.

The remainder of the day passed with little excitement, at least not in comparison to how it started. People came in and orders went out. It was the same humdrum existence that had plagued her since childhood. She caught herself drifting off from time to time, wondering what role she might play in her father's plan. She fantasized that this might be the day she proved herself to the council. After all, if there was something her father could not do without her, then she must be some use. She ran through possibility after possibility on her drive home. She could not possibly call her father and ask. She did not want to seem desperate or power hungry. No, she must wait and let the situation run its course. She must be patient.

It seemed like it took an hour to get to her house. It was a small place but served its purpose. She had been offered a portion of land on her family's property but turned it down. There were times that she regretted the decision now. How easy would it have been, she wondered, to just take the help that she was offered? She remembered very clearly why she said no.

In Blair County, Wittlich was synonymous with privilege. Toriana had fought tooth and nail to shrug off the preconceived notion of her being a spoiled little princess. She allowed her father to do very little for her except when he extended the offer for her to run the day-to-day operations of the family business. She accepted the opportunity more as a matter of necessity. She spent her upbringing in that shop. She knew it inside and out. In fact, it was all she knew. There was no one who would run it better and nothing she would do better than run it.

After graduating high school, she first had an apartment in town until she saved up enough money to buy her little house in the woods. It was a dream for her then. It was secluded, cozy, and small enough that upkeep was relatively easy. She felt a sense of familiar relief pulling into the driveway to her sanctuary.

As was her routine, she pulled off her boots on the front porch, unlocked the door, placed her bag and keys on the entryway table and collapsed onto the couch. She paid no mind to the television remote resting on the chair arm. Her mind was still abuzz. It was almost as if she dozed for a minute; falling into a dream like state of retreat. She was startled back to reality by a sense of someone at the door. Just then came a soft, familiar knock.

It was Evan - she could smell him. His scent was equal parts perspiration from effort and sweet manly drive. Beneath it all was a note of leather from something she could not put her finger on. She assumed it was from his boots until she discovered its presence prevailed even when he wore nothing at all.

Toriana could not sense her feet striking the floor as she walked to the doorway. It was as if she floated. Turning the knob, she felt a lump rise into her throat. Unexplainable nervousness had churned up and blocked the vocal chords from flexing to form words. As she got to the door, she saw only his hand at first. It was as if she was seeing him in sections, as the growing gap between door and doorframe exposed him more. Before she could will herself to speak, Evan began to explain his visit.

"Your father suggested I apologize," he said.

Toriana felt vindicated and exceedingly confident knowing that he was now on her turf on her terms. She stepped to the side of the door and stretched out her hand to point into the living room. Evan was not sure if this was a friendly invitation inside or an order to enter. He obliged either way. Toriana closed the door behind her but remained near it. Evan had already walked to the center of the room and had turned to face her.

Evan asked, "Are we going to sit and discuss this or are you going to stand there and wait for me to gravel at your feet."

Tersely, she responded, "Since there is not much to discuss, I suppose you could save us a lot of time and jump directly to option two."

Although Evan knew to expect such a response, he could not help but feel the full sting of this slap. Unable to bear it any longer, he began to pour out.

"I know you don't need me. I get it. But this isn't the way it has to be", he started. Before Toriana could shake her shock and reply, Evan began to walk toward her. Stopping barely a foot away from her, he said softly, "You can stop proving your point." He inched closer. Now his hand was on the side of her face. Her eyes rose to meet his and just before pressing his lips into hers, he breathed, "There is only one thing I can give you that you cannot give yourself. So you might as well let me."

He pressed into her roughly. She backed up to the door to give her a solid foundation. She wanted to feel all of him and every ounce of pressure that he held against her. She felt her skin flush and her heart and lungs swell as her bestial attributes responded to his touch. Her sense of smell sharpened and she breathed in familiar leather. She could feel Evan's muscles tense and engorge. Lust fueled partial shift in them both. As Evan grew in size, his clothing began to rip and fall away.

He drew away from her slightly and took a second to survey her expression. Her face was turned up toward the ceiling, as if in prayer, and her neck was fully exposed. He placed his hand at the center of her neck and traced down to the button of her blue jeans. She felt her skin tingle, as blood rushed to follow his touch. He placed his fingertips in the waistband of her jeans and made a fist, tearing them away from her body at the seams. Evan curled his forearm beneath her rear and easily lifted her with one arm.

Face to face now, she traced his lips with her tongue and wrapped her legs and arms around his torso. She felt her body cave to the will of his passion and allowed him inside. He let out a satisfied moan and she followed in kind. Rhythmically they writhed together against the door; him savoring every pulse and her gripping him tighter as she neared release. Dropping her face into the curve of his neck, a rush of pleasure ran over her. She could feel his pulse rise as each thrust became more vigorous than the last. They shivered together. She lost her strength.

Evan held Toriana to him. Cradling her in his arms, he walked to her bedroom and laid her in bed. He found his place beside her. He watched her in silence for a while, marveling at the softness in her face. Her eyes were closed and the corners of her mouth were curled in what could have easily become a smile. There was no tension in her outstretched hands or furrow in her brow. She was so still and statuesque that it startled him when her eyes began to open.

Evan nervously quipped, "Well, that ought to fix your attitude, at least for a little while." He cut his eyes toward her with a half smile, hoping to gauge her reaction. Toriana burst into laughter. It was a loud hearty laugh that trailed off into schoolgirl giggle. An involuntary grin grew across Evan's face and without realizing it he whispered, "That's my girl."

Toriana quickly replied, "Your girl...you must be joking."

Evan knew he had just potentially stepped into the lion's den and had to recover quickly.

"Come on, Tori, princess hardass or not, even you have to admit we weren't so bad together" he said.

Toriana agreed with the assessment 'not so bad'. She explained, "When I like you, I am crazy about you, and when I don't like you, I can't stand you. I just don't think that one is worth the other. Besides, I do pretty well on my own."

"Do you?"

"Do I what?"

"Do pretty well on your own?"

"What, don't I seem like it?"

"I'm not asking what it seems like, I am asking for a direct answer to a direction question."

"What difference does it make?"

Toriana's response left Evan frustrated and confused. He would never understand how she could so obstinately refuse to let anyone in. How could she snub him? Evan had tired with the game and, having nothing else to say, simply replied.

"That's my cue."

Toriana did not understand his meaning until he stood up to walk out the door. She knew that being naked would not stop him from going to his truck and driving home.

"Wow", Toriana said, "you really are an overgrown child, aren't you?"

"It's not worth it anymore, Tori," Evan said defeated. "Until you figure out that being heartless isn't going to get you respect, there is nothing I can say to you. Having a soul isn't a sign of weakness. Whether you like it or not I care about you I..." he trailed off, short of finishing his thought.

He stared at her waiting for a reaction. The stoniness in her stare never eased. Her eyes never diverted from the spot where he had been until she heard his truck pull away. Her face fell into her hands. Numb, she could only replay his words in her mind. Heartless and soulless were not words she had ever associated with herself. In retrospect, however, what else could she be called? She had done this. As a matter of fact, she had spent years perfecting the art of being this. "No attachments, no strings, no issues", she used to say. She was a fool; a heartless, soulless fool. Alone she had built this prison and alone that night she slept.

After a fitful night, she rose, no less drained and with no more answers. She got to the shop on autopilot and started to work in the same fashion. Between fake smiles to customers, she sat at her desk hoping the phone would ring. Her cell phone sat on her desk, halting any chance of productivity. She had no idea what she would say the next time she spoke to Evan. If she apologized would he even believe her?

After having all but giving up, the phone screen suddenly illuminated and she grabbed it with such a fury that it almost slid to the floor. Finally figuring out which end was up, she read the screen. It was Dietrich.

"Good morning daddy", she answered.

"Hello, sweetheart. I was thinking that I would come by the shop around closing and pick you up for the meeting. If don't mind riding with an old man."

Toriana laughed and said she would love to. Hanging up, she sighed. She was happy for the interruption and oddly relieved. She wished she could just pull the trigger and be the one to make the first call. Fear, however, had a solid hold on her. Sitting at her desk, she stretched her arms above her, closed her eyes, and took a deep, deliberate breath. She had to focus. Until her father's call, she had almost forgotten how important the night ahead could be to her future.

She spent the remainder of the day taking a mental inventory of every conflict and resolution that she had witnessed in the hoard over her lifetime. How would she have done it different? What could she possibly have contributed? She practiced speeches and she paced the length of her office. Her boots struck the floor at a steady pace, acting as a metronome for her words. S

he began to hear a second set of boots approaching the door and hurriedly sat behind her desk. Dietrich walked in without knocking, as she knew he would. She rose to greet her father with a warm hug. As they pulled away, he rested his hand on her shoulder and spoke quietly.

"How about a rundown of how things are going around here?"

She smiled and stretched out her hand as if to say "after you". She knew that her father had no interest in the day-to-day affairs of the shop. He simply wanted to walk around the empire that he had built and marvel at it. She let him lead their path, as she had always done. Dietrich spoke.

"I remember how important this place was to you, even as a tiny thing. Especially after we lost your mother."

Toriana remembered it as well. She was her father's sidekick then. She clung to his every word and imitated his every move. She would stretch her legs out as far as they would go trying to trace his footsteps with her own. As a young child, she saw the shop as more of a candy land than a business. She rambled from table to table and rack to rack, taking a bite here and a nibble there. She remembered the day her father caught her. He crouched down to meet her face and calmly explained, "This is food but it isn't for us. It isn't ours because we didn't hunt it. We didn't earn it. You should only take what you hunt and only hunt as much as you need. We share the land with other packs and with the humans. It is important that we respect those relationships." She never snuck another morsel.

Fracturing the silence, she asked her father, "Is there anything I need to know for tonight. I mean anything I need to prepare for?"

"I wouldn't worry about your part of it too much, dear. We are just going to have to redistribute some territory. That is all there is to it. It's the only way to keep the peace. Adrian and Leo are certainly not going to resolve it themselves, stubborn old bastards. You know how it goes with those two. I may need some back up, that is all. The more help I have explaining my point, the better."

Toriana smiled at her father's confidence in her. He was right. He would need all the help he could get. The Krams and

Klein families had been a single entity for some time. It was only recently that Adrian Krams decided to pull his family out of the arrangement, although it was long in making. During the mass exodus of packs from Germany, many families found themselves at risk of being left behind. They simply could not afford to make the journey. Many struck deals with surrounding packs to gather funds. Some sold assets and others, in essence, sold themselves.

The Kleins provided transport to the Krams pack in exchange for labor once both packs had safely arrived in the States. In the beginning, both packs prospered under the agreement. The Kleins used their substantial estate to buy land and fund infrastructure. The Krams were skilled tradesmen, erecting massive barns and palatial homes and later maintaining huge amounts of livestock. The Krams women provided domestic services and had an enviable hand at textiles. Many years passed this way; the Krams pack laboring and the Klein pack enjoying the fruits. Finally, the inevitable came.

The leaders of the Krams pack requested the balance due, of sorts, on their journey to America. The Kleins refused to provide the information and relations between the packs chilled. The Krams' began demanding payment for their labor and the Kleins slowly whittled away the hunting grounds that had been designated for Krams use for so many years. It wasn't until Adrian Krams, the pack's current leader, rose to power that the pack out right demanded reparation under threat of all out war.

The council was forced to step in and hunting grounds were distributed between the packs. That distribution was now, once again, in question.

Toriana was thrilled at her time to shine. She settled onto a stool across from her father and basked in the glow of her upward mobility and position of trust. It was, however, only momentary.

As if suddenly remembering her, Dietrich asked, "Oh, did Evan get around to speaking to you yet?"

Toriana struggled to hold a flush from her face and nervous sweat rose on her neck as she remembered the night before. Her father had no reason to suspect her embarrassment, but she nevertheless feared giving herself away. She nodded.

"Good," Dietrich said, "He is a fine young man. All young man act a bit like him, for better or worse, but he's a fine one, regardless. You should really give him his due, dear. He's been a loyal ally to this family for years and, if it wasn't for him, things might not be so amicable between the Fahrenholz pack and us. His father is a difficult man to talk to, on his best day."

Toriana chuckled a little inside at her father's request for her to give Evan his due. She angled herself away from Dietrich's sight to hide a guilty smile and hummed, "Fine is one way to describe him."

Rising to his feet, Dietrich clapped Toriana on the back and said, "I suppose we had better get going. Most of those old codgers are on the edge of death anyway. No sense in wasting what little time they have left. They just haven't managed to age as well as your daddy." He winked and wrapped his arm around her shoulder as they left the shop.

They drove to the council house in near silence. Toriana rode, preoccupied with rehearsing to herself. One had to know the county very well to find the council house. It was a secluded cabin, far off of the beaten path. Not accessible by anything without four-wheel drive, it's position and geography made it ideal for conducting business away from the prying eyes of outsiders.

Beyond heavy, wooden, double doors sat a large round table and gallery of chairs. Nicotine stains still clung to the walls in memory of the days before the much-challenged ban on smoking in the building. A rabble of voices hummed inside single room cabin. Despite their early departure, it appeared as if the Wittlich's were the last to arrive. The men of the hoard were everywhere. Ranging from the overall-clad to those who would not dare be seen at such a function without wearing a suit, every pack was represented.

Nearest the door were the Bedburgs, an enterprising pack who had made a small fortune off of various real estate and ranch sales. Cell phone coverage was spotty at the council house, so it paid to be close to the door and windows if one was wishing to have full use of his or her smartphone. Clause Bedburg served as both the president of Bedburg Properties and the leader of the Bedburg clan. For the Bedburgs, business and family were one in the same. Frank, the patriarch of the Fahrenholz pack and Evan's father, stood near the back of the room. He was accompanied by his brothers Brandon and Jacob, as well as a few members of other packs. Frank and his brothers typically showed up for appearances sake. It was rare that they bring anything up for council consideration. Frank tended to err on the side of being more reactive than proactive.

He and his pack lived like most of the human families in Blair County. They owned and operated a family ranch that did little more than sustain them, attended the local Church of Christ regularly, and were a staple at community events. Frank believed in Jesus, hard work, and being a man of character.

Then, of course were the Krams' and the Kleins. Situated on either side of the room, it was clear that they had already drawn battle lines. Dietrich had a talent at these events. Everyone knew him, everyone respected him, and everyone scuttled to have an opportunity at his ear. Toriana was both intrigued and humored by it. It was a bit like watching clamoring fans at the feet of some hotshot A-lister. She chuckled at the comparison.

In her mind, her father was a man like any other. Although she respected him and admired him immensely, she could never seem to understand how grown men could be star struck by him. Toriana remained mostly invisible. Being the only woman in the room should have made her stand out, but, in keeping with usual practices, everyone ignored her presence to prevent having to address it. Had anyone else brought a female pack member to Council, they would have been shunned immediately. Dietrich, however, seemed to be immune from all such scrutiny.

Suddenly an anonymous voice rose above the crowd calling for the meeting to begin. As was tradition, pack leaders settled into their seats around the table. Many years ago, pack leaders had decided that there would be no set leadership at council meetings. They feared that by designating one person to lead the meeting, that other packs would not be given fair time to address grievances. The system worked well, except for the first few moments of each council, where pack leaders would usually look across the table from each other in silence waiting on someone to start.

Finally, Clause spoke up, saying, "I think that we should first address the Fahrenholz incident last Halloween." Clause waited a moment for someone to protest before continuing.

"Frank, novel idea to shift in front of the children at the church haunted house. However, a little forethought and discretion would be appreciated before another such stunt."

Frank snickered. Clause could be depended upon to bring up behavioral issues. While every pack leader was concerned about the hoard being found out, Clause was particularly sensitive. It was common consensus among pack leaders that he was embarrassed of his kind.

Leo Kleine spoke next. "I'm inclined to agree with Clause. It was funny and all, Frank, but we really do not need people getting curious. Ya know?"

Frank, always the first to admit he was wrong, said, "Okay, I'll admit it wasn't the best idea. Won't happen again." Frank's still present smirk indicated that he regretted nothing. However, knowing Frank to be a man of his word, the hoard was satisfied with the response.

Leo, still having the floor, continued. "While we are on the subject of staying low key, I'm not thrilled with what I've been hearing about the Bedburgs leasing out their hunting grounds to human hunters."

Clause defended himself immediately, saying, "Lets get some things clear. Firstly, I've not actually leased my grounds out to anyone. We are still weighing our options on it. Secondly, even if we did, they are our hunting grounds and we should be able to use them as we please. They were allocated to us and..."

Clause found himself cut off by Adrian Krams asking "Are we going to avoid the elephant in the room indefinitely? Because if that is the case, I'm just going to go ahead and leave."

It sounded a bit like a tantrum. Nevertheless, Toriana sat silently cheering Adrian on. His protests, she just knew, would be the springboard she needed to launch her into a position of respectability among the elders. She inched closer to the edge of her chair, hoping it would not creak. She sat up taller and swallowed hard to wet her throat. She could not risk her voice cracking when the moment came.

Dietrich spoke first, saying, "Adrian, is there something bothering you?".

Adrian's attention snapped toward Dietrich and he said, "Damn right there is. We have two packs here who have waited months to be heard. I will not continue to be ignored while you all bicker about Clause's greed and Frank's silly parlor tricks."

"Alright then, Adrian," Frank said, taking offense to being called silly, "what of it?"

Adrian went on with his grievances.

"Last year, when Leo and I parted ways, this bunch here, in all of it's infinite knowledge, decided to split up our lands to your liking."

Frank had nearly all he could take of being berated by Adrian and interrupted the mud slinging, saying, "Now hold on, Adrian. We had to do something. We couldn't just let your little pissing match spring into an all out war."

Dietrich, fulfilling his role as diplomat interrupted.

"Frank, let him be heard."

Frank settled back into his chair, heading Dietrich's request. Adrian glared at Frank in contempt, then redirected his attention to the group and continued.

"Since that decision was made, both packs have suffered. Neither parcel of land can accommodate game year round. In the winter my pack struggles and in the summer, I assume, Leo feels the same pressure."

Leo nodded in agreement.

"We agree on little besides that we want the best for our packs, just as any man here," Adrian concluded.

Frank spoke again, asking, " What do you suggest, Adrian?"

Adrian dropped his head in defeat, and said with a sigh, "I only know that I am tired of the fight. I've lost my taste for it. But I cannot and will not be under Leo Klein's thumb any longer."

The room fell silent, every man in it feeling Adrian's shame. Toriana looked at her father, waiting for the signal to speak. She had no notion of what to say. Both excitement and panic ran through her until Dietrich's voice shattered the silence.

"Might I offer a suggestion?" he asked. Every man's attention belonged to Dietrich alone, which he took as a green light to continue.

"I've had a great deal of time to think about this. Everyone here agrees that we do not want war between packs. It would be messy and possibly deadly to us all. I, as a father of a pack, know the importance of doing what is best for our own and that there isn't one of us who would want our fates decided for us." he said.

Toriana looked around the room. The men reminded her of dashboard dogs as they all nodded, nearly in unison. Though it was slightly comical, Toriana was too caught up in the tension of impatiently waiting for her father's next words to laugh.

Dietrich continued, saying, "I propose a temporary fix, to give each family some relief until they can come up with a permanent solution on their own."

Toriana was unclear of her father's direction on this. She had assumed that there would be new territory lines negotiated and agreed upon. It appeared that Dietrich was going with a new game plan entirely. Dietrich continued.

"I propose that, for one year, each pack has unlimited access to the entirety of the territory, with the exception of residential areas, and alternate use quarterly. By alternating four times a year, each pack has plenty of opportunity to gather game and feed their packs for the year. "

Adrian spoke up, saying, "This is all well and good. But how are we supposed to make sure everyone is playing fair?"

Dietrich answered, "I would be willing to hold temporary control over the territory to ensure that the agreement is kept."

Toriana marveled at her father's brilliance. However, Adrian immediately objected.

"I did not spend the better part of my life fighting to have what was rightfully mine to hand it over to someone else..."

Leo stopped Adrian's rant short. Leo turned to Dietrich and asked, "If we were to go along with this arrangement, how could you guarantee that you would be impartial? Hell, how do we know you will release the territory back to us once this is all sorted out?"

"Exactly!" Adrian added.

Dietrich opened his mouth but did not speak for a moment. He then said, "I would be willing to send my daughter, Toriana, to live with one of the packs to ensure that no ill will is intended."

Toriana jumped up from her chair but could not speak for her outrage. The entire room, with the exception of Dietrich, looked at her.

Before she could speak, Leo looked at Adrian and said, "As stubborn as we are, this may be the only solution. I would be willing to allow her to stay with you and your huntresses. Dietrich, is this agreeable to you?"

Toriana shouted at her father.

"No, daddy, this is not agreeable to you. Stop this."

Dietrich turned away from her and nodded yes. Toriana was stunned and enraged. She turned to address the room.

"I don't give a shit who agrees to what. It is not going to happen. I'm not for sale, trade, or anything else and I will *not* be sent to Adrian's little slave force."

Dietrich stood, stepping closely to his daughter's face and spoke softly. Toriana could make out something about it only being one year but could hardly hear him over the hum in the room. She lashed out at her father.

"How could you even think of this? Are you going crazy in your old age..."

Dietrich took his daughter's arm, freighting her into silence. Toriana had never seen such anger in her father's eyes. His voice thundered at her.

"You are a member of this pack and will be loyal. I am done with your repeated insubordination. This is happening."

Dietrich caught himself and let go of her arm. He sat down, appearing to have startled even himself. He sat up tall and did not take his eyes off of Toriana. Toriana bent down and fought tears as she spoke to her father.

"You are the disloyal one. You have no real power. You are nothing but an impotent and stupid man."

She turned away and walked out of the door. It hurt Toriana to say it more than it could have ever hurt her father to hear it.

Toriana went to the parking area, her view of her father entirely shattered. She had no idea what to do next. Where would she go? The question more pressing at the moment was how would she get there? She pulled her phone from her pocket and dialed Evan. She did not know if she was calling for help or to tell him goodbye. She thought she would decide when she heard his voice. The phone rang three, four, six times until his voice mail picked up. She called several more times. Finally, she accepted that he had finally gotten tired of the abuse. He didn't care if she needed him or wanted him.

Inside, the group was quiet. Adrian looked at Dietrich, waiting on him to change his mind. Dietrich was looking at the floor, hiding tears as he instructed Adrian to take her. Toriana heard several men approaching and took the woods for concealment. Still undecided of her next move, and by now panicking, she seemed to be pacing. Never having heard the stealthy elder werewolves approaching, she quickly found herself surrounded. She began to shift, determined to fend them off. She heard Adrian behind her.

"Tori, if you fight you will be torn apart. You know you are just a child. You are not as strong or as skilled as we are and we do not want to do this."

Toriana knew that he was right. Her only chance for survival was to comply, at least for the moment. She gave up, followed Adrian to his truck and wedged herself between other nameless members of his pack in the back seat. Toriana steeled herself and her pride, refusing to cry. She was staring out the window when she noticed her father. He was unloading a suitcase from his truck and handing it to Adrian. It was her suitcase.

In that moment, Toriana understood what her father meant by needing her help. She felt foolish and betrayed. She took one last look at his face, knowing it would probably be the last. She silently said goodbye to her pack, her dreams, and life as she knew it. She said goodbye to her world. She knew that things would never be the same.

*****

Toriana did not speak on the way to the Krams homestead. She could not form intelligible sentences in her fractured mind. She wondered where exactly she was going, what she would be doing, how she would escape and why her father had done this. What had she done to deserve this? Was it her fault at all? She feared there would always be more questions than answers.

She knew that she would likely never speak to her father again. If she was unable to find a means of escape, she had no doubt he would secure her freedom at the end of a year as promised. She could not understand why she still clung to the fact that he would keep his word. He had betrayed her in a way that she could never have imagined. He had stripped her of everything she had ever fought for. Any sense of self or security was snatched away in an instant.

Although Toriana hardly noticed, no one else in the truck spoke much either. She occasionally caught them exchanging glances with each other. She saw a look of concern, as if they were worried how she might react. It was little consolation, under the circumstances, but she enjoyed being able to make them nervous. They had good reason to be. When they first embarked, she had entertained the notion of incapacitating the driver and running. It was a short-lived plan. She knew that she was overpowered. There were four men in the vehicle; two old and two young. The agility, strength, and stamina of the young men were not her primary concern. She feared the experience and precision of the two older men. They had spent decades on the hunt and had honed their skills in tracking.

It was difficult to swallow that a werewolf would "tear apart" one of their own, as they had threatened, but she did not underestimate the ferocity with which these men might protect their pack. Her only option, she concluded, was to find an opportunity to disappear. Whether she would wait for it or create it, she had not yet decided.

She was shaken alert when they crossed the cattle guard at the entrance of the homestead. She had never been here. Strangely, she had never known anyone outside of the Krams and Kleine packs who had. The cedars around the cattle guard created something akin to a corridor. It went on for several hundred feet before opening up to a nearly barren field. They continued to travel a well-worn dirt path that skirted the pasture in an easterly direction. She could see lights in the distance and assumed that they were an indication of her destination. She paid close attention to the route, trying to mentally annotate each turn and clump of trees along the way. The county had fallen into darkness by then, making it no easy task. She wanted to survey the stars for direction, just as her father had taught her to do but could not angle herself toward the window for the young men situated on either side. She could have leaned over them but did not want to give her tactics away. Besides that was the fact that she did not want to touch them any more than she was already forced to. She was disgusted with them. They were her captors, her mortal enemies. She had already resolved that if ever given the chance, she would dismantle their lives, piece by piece.

The journey concluded at a large residence. It reminded Toriana of one of the plantation style homes that were scattered around the county. She was always a little saddened when she drove by the ones that had long since been abandoned and allowed to rot. This one, however, was remarkably well appointed. It had a large wrap around porch, dotted with chairs, and, beyond the porch, on both floors, were dozens of windows. Light shined from behind several, illuminating what appeared to be bedrooms. There were so many bedrooms. She could make out the shadows of young women as they gathered around the windows to greet the approaching headlights.

She had heard tales of the huntresses. They were the kind of stories that circulate around any small community: part truth, part fantasy, part horror. There were stories of women being chained and beaten. Others, mostly the old men, thought of them as a pseudo-utopian style group of beauties, who loved nothing more than taking care of the men of the pack. Then there were depictions of them as hideous beasts that ravenously and brutally sought out game. The adolescent boys, of course, weighed in, crafting fantasies of a pack of loincloth clad lesbians who spent their days hunting and their nights engaged in orgies.

She had never given any of them much credence. They were, nevertheless, the only basis on which she had to form an impression of the situation and had embedded themselves in her mind.

The truck halted directly in front of the main door. All of her co-passengers poured out and she followed suit. The men, all but Adrian, moved into a huddle at the back of the pickup. Toriana assumed they were exchanging opinions on the night's events. They were saying things that they were too cowardly to say in her presence.

Adrian retrieved Toriana's bag from the bed of the truck and tried to hand it to her. She coldly stared at him and allowed it to drop to the ground. Adrian stared at the bag and took a deep breath.

Gathering himself, Adrian said, "Toriana, you are not a slave here. Please do not expect to be treated badly. That being said, do not expect to be treated like daddy's little princess either. While you are here, however long it may be, you will be expected to work, just like everyone else."

Despite the rage welling inside of her, Toriana never flinched. She did not speak, did not frown, did not do anything to betray her pride. Her pride, what little remained, was all she had left. Adrian and Toriana remained deadlocked in a silent battle of wills for a moment. Adrian disengaged first and went back to the truck where the other men were already seated. As they drove away, Adrian's words replayed in her mind. He had called her "daddy's little princess". She balked at the irony, unable to let it go. Nearly every decision she had made in her adult life was aimed at avoiding this characterization. In the end, however, it was her father's decision that made it very clear she was no princess of his.

Toriana remained on the lawn of the huntress' lair. She could feel the eyes of the women inside pulling at her. She would not be intimidated. Regardless of the stories that circulated about them, there was one undeniable truth about these women. They were at the bottom of the bottom of the Krams hierarchy.

While under the ownership of the Kleine pack, the concept of servitude and class separation became deeply ingrained into the Krams and the way in which they conducted pack affairs. The patriarchal nature of the pack secured women as the powerless and the inevitable target for servitude. The women became responsible for all domestic needs, as well as providing food for the pack. Men in the Krams pack only hunted for sport. Werewolves could survive on small animals but needed large amounts of red meat to stay healthy. The huntresses were tasked with fulfilling those needs for the men of the pack. It was a nearly endless job.

Toriana both pitied and despised these women. How could they allow themselves to be held under the thumb of men? Did they not know to fight? Were they that ignorant?

She heard a voice from the dark, "Are you going to come inside?" The voice was soft but beneath the tone Toriana could detect a note of sarcasm. It was almost if the actual question asked was "Are you going to stand out here and talk to yourself for the rest of the night?"

Toriana walked toward the voice and its creator came into view. She was tall and so thin that she could have easily have been mistaken for frail. Her long hair cascaded over one shoulder and Toriana could see red intermingled with the blonde. The figure took several long steps to meet Toriana. She stopped and stuck out one hand and introduced herself as Lisa. The women walked up the steps and onto the porch together. As they approached the door, Lisa opened it and motioned for Toriana to step inside ahead of her. Toriana hesitated briefly; the old wives tales were suddenly at the forefront of her mind. Shaking them off, she stepped on inside.

Beyond the front door, Toriana found that the women who had moments ago occupied the windows were gone. The main foyer was abandoned. To her left she could see an archway leading to a large parlor. The furnishings transcended time. It looked like a flea market where furniture and accents from the last 50 years of trends had found themselves amassed together. There were floral couches, shag rugs, and a few beanbag chairs for good measure.

"Yeah", Lisa acknowledged, "we get the old stuff that comes out of the other houses." "There is an empty room in the back. It's quiet. Would you like it?" Lisa continued.

Toriana, still surveying the oddities in the main parlor, replied faintly "Won't need it. I'm not staying long."

Lisa, intrigued and startled by the statement, delivered an exaggerated nod. She cut her eyes back and forth across the scratched wooden floor as if searching for a reply.

"Look," she said "You are pissed and I understand that but take it from me, whatever you are planning, ain't gonna work out."

Toriana became instantly livid.

"And who are you to tell me what is and isn't going to work?" she snarled.

Lisa stepped backwards, not from fear but as an act of self-restraint. She cleared her throat calmly.

"You don't know how this place works. I do. The asshole brigade keeps us under constant watch and all it takes is once."

"Once for what" Toriana asked apprehensively.

Lisa took her by the arm and walked her swiftly into the parlor. Both women were nearly at a trot when they stopped beneath the light of a disgustingly ornate floor lamp. Lisa wiggled her right arm out of her shirtsleeve and maneuvered the rest of the garment up around her shoulder. Toriana first noticed jagged scars on Lisa's upper arm. In her mind she whispered "claw marks" but hoped that the words did not find their way out. Beyond them, spanning Lisa's shoulders, were deeply gouges. They were healed but pink nonetheless. Radiating from each gouge were many smaller marks, permanently peppering Lisa's flesh. Lisa heard Toriana gasp before Toriana realized she had.

Working her shirt back into place Lisa said, "See? Bad idea."

Toriana collapsed into an armchair. Lisa lit a cigarette and situated herself on the floor a few feet away. Lisa started again.

"They take care of things 'the old way' around here. It's like a little reminder of how much worse it was back in the old country. The quick and dirty version of my story is that I ran, they caught me, I fought, they won, and then they proceeded to peel chunks out of my back with pliers until they thought I'd learned my lesson."

Toriana opened her mouth and, before she knew it, "How does everyone not know about this?!" feel out. Lisa chuckled cryptically.

"The great and powerful Adrian considers it a family affair. Besides, who are we gonna tell?" she said, smiling at her own pitiful joke. Toriana was still in a daze.

Lisa asked, "What did you think went on here anyway?"

Toriana replied, "Truthfully, I just assumed that you were all ignorant little housewives. I guess I figured you all lacked the gumption to do anything about any of it. I sure as hell didn't know about this."

Lisa continued to laugh and said, "Well, we do have some dumb bitches, but that isn't why we are here. If I remember correctly, I won my trip to huntress-ville by being a willful little smart ass."

Lisa could see the question burning in Toriana's eyes and answered it before it was asked.

"Some of the girls got here because they couldn't keep their legs closed, some because they couldn't keep their mouths closed, and others just didn't want to play the game anymore. We are difficult, they say. So difficult, in fact, that we had to be sent away to learn something about respect. So we are kept here to work our asses off for the benefit of everyone else. Great gig, huh?"

She took a long drag off of her cigarette and snuffed it out in a bronze jewelry box. Toriana suddenly felt a need to reply with some kind of substance.

"So I guess you don't know what happened to me then?"

Lisa replied, "We might not get out much but we don't live under a rock."

Toriana was relieved by not having to recount the story. She was still a bit fuzzy on the details. Everything seemed to have happened in the blink of an eye. Lisa stood and walked back into the foyer. She snatched Toriana's bag to the floor and disappeared into a long hallway. Toriana hurried to follow. At the end of the hall, Lisa pushed open a door and unceremoniously tossed the bag inside.

"There is your room," she said. "The quiet one."

Toriana pondered how to express her appreciation but never got the chance to decide. Lisa, again, took her by the arm and led her in yet another direction. Without turning to look at her, Lisa spoke up.

"I suppose you should meet the other girls."

Lisa passed several doors before turning sharply to face her intended target. She knocked aggressively and, upon receiving no answer, spoke in a loud, authoritative voice.

"I know you bitches are up. You've been listening through the door the whole time."

She flashed a mischievous smile at Toriana. The door opened and behind it stood three twenty-somethings in a huddle. Ever the diplomat, Lisa began the introductions.

"Tori, its cool if I call you Tori, right? Tori, this is Maggie, Arlene, and April."

The three stood silent for a moment. Maggie was glaring cross-armed at Lisa.

"Well, ladies, won't you invite us in for a chat?" Lisa asked with a mock curtsy.

She wound her arm around Toriana's and walked them both inside. Toriana felt outnumbered and a bit intimidated. She was not accustomed to keeping the company of other women. She hadn't avoided it. The opportunity simply had seldom availed itself in her lifetime. Lisa plopped down cross-legged on the floor, as appeared to be her habit. Once again, Lisa had the floor.

"Well, let's all get acquainted then, shall we? I'm a bitch, Maggie is a whore, April is a dyke, Arlene likes to hack on herself, and Tori here is a bargaining chip."

No one argued. It seemed as if they had already come to terms with their labels. Toriana found herself staring at Arlene. She noticed that the girl was covered in scars and clutching a teddy bear. As a matter of fact, everything about her was childlike.

"M..m..my parents couldn't really handle my...um..my..thing. So they decided it would be best if I came here and learned some toughness," Arlene stuttered.

Toriana could only nod and look to the others to save her from the awkwardness of being caught.

Maggie finally asked, "So is it true? Did your dad really just trade you off?"

Toriana felt her heart sink a little. With no other option than the truth, she answered, "Yeah, pretty close. The details aren't really that important anyway."

She felt an odd sense of solidarity with the women, having admitted her position. She didn't let it linger long.

"So is this it? I mean us. Are we the only ones?" she asked.

"No," April answered, "There are 13 more up and down these halls. But we're the good ones."

The rest of the girls continued to cackle. Toriana drifted into silence, wondering if this was what was to be for her. She nearly resigned herself to the fact that this gaggle of misfits would become her home.

"Guys," Toriana said, "I think I'm gonna head to bed. This has been one hell of a day."

She exited and wound her way to her appointed room. Without bothering to turn on the light, she curled up on the bed. As her eyes involuntarily closed, her thoughts found their way to anger, shame, fear, resentment, and loneliness. She thought about her father but mostly she thought about Evan. Fortunately, her half sleeping brain would not allow her to focus for long. Finally, she slept.

She was woken from a much deeper sleep than expected by man's voice. The voice was accompanied by the hard crashes of several pairs of boots down the hallway. The sounds were close, too close. There was a pounding on the other side of her bedroom door. She stood out of bed and went for the door. The knocking continued until she interrupted it by removing the door from the fist's reach. A tall, muscular man stood framed in the doorway. He peered at her as if he were unsure of what he was seeing. She didn't recognize the man, but he clearly recognized here.

"Yeah?" Toriana groggily sighed.

The man smirked and placed his hand on his hips.

"Well, Princess Wittlich, welcome to the team. Get your shit together, we gotta get moving."

As unceremoniously as he arrived, he turned and walked back down the hallway into the main foyer. He began to yell, in an almost celebratory tone, the countdown to departure. He started at the 10-minute mark. Toriana, still a bit lost in her new surroundings, leaned out of the doorway and looked around for any indication of the location of the washroom. Girls, in various stages of dress, funneled past the foyer and toward another hall. She tore into her bag hoping that all of her personal items would be there. She had not thought to check it. She found her toothbrush, toothpaste, shower items, deodorant, and all of the other necessary toiletries. She also found her favorite hairbrush, a silver-plated boar's hair antique given to her after her mother's passing, tucked gently in a corner of the bag.

She was momentarily thankful for her father's gentle attention in selecting this particular item to pack. She held it for a moment and crouched on the floor, allowing it to fall into her lap. Her head hung and he eyes began to tear. She was rattled out of the moment by the call "7 minutes, girls!"

Toriana, with items spilling out of her arms, followed the flow of women into an open bedroom with an attached bathroom. There was a line going into the bathroom. Toriana asked a blonde woman next to her what the line was all about.

"There are two stalls for all of us. Which means you probably won't get a shower...newbie."

Toriana was irritated with the woman's attitude but knew she was probably right. She looked around for a possible solution. She noticed that the far wall of the bedroom had been outfitted with several sinks, one of which was empty. She went to the sink and remembered she had not grabbed a towel. She missed her little home in the woods already. She stripped off her shirt and placed it under the running water. She wiped herself down quickly and brushed her teeth. She pulled her soaked shirt back, re-gathered her belongings, and weaved back though the mass of women to her room.

Crossing the foyer she passed a man who crudely crooned "wet t-shirt time." Toriana stopped in her tracks. She felt embarrassment, followed by a sharp rush of anger run up her body. She turned and approached him. She stepped directly in front of him, so closely that she found herself looking up at his considerable height.

Her brow tightly furrowed, she asked "Who the hell are you?"

"Daniel" he answered. Daniel was not fazed by her boldness or apparent anger. He only smirked and went back to standing as he had been. Toriana surveyed him carefully, looking at him long enough to notice that his hazel eyes had a thin line of yellow around the irises. She was waiting for any sign that he was uncomfortable or intimidated. He showed none, only smirking at her, as if asking a question.

She defiantly huffed and said, "Good to know who I'm dealing with." She could feel his eyes following her as she walked back to her room. Once inside, she opened the closet to throw her bag inside. She laughed a bit as she saw the contents of the closet. Inside were linens, extra pillows, and towels. It was almost like a hotel. She wondered how routine it must have been for these people to throw away their daughters.

She heard Daniel's alarm of "One minute, ladies." She wasn't quite sure what it meant but certainly understood that she should be doing something. She walked back into the foyer where the found the rest of the huntresses gathered. She was now one of them. They were mostly dressed in old t-shirts and blue jeans. Their clothing was far from rags but definitely worse for the wear. Many of the items looked like they had been brought to the huntress house when the wearer was deposited there. Other items looked like hand me downs that found their way from woman to woman over the years.

The blonde from the bathroom pushed passed Toriana, nudging her shoulder intentionally. She turned the scowl at her but was stopped by a much more welcome face - Lisa.

Without Toriana asking the question, Lisa said, "That's Amber. She's a bitch and we all know it. She's gonna get her ass kicked one day. But not today, all right killer?" She laughed and put her arm around Toriana as the huntresses filed behind Daniel and out the door.

Once outside, the huntresses separated into groups and loaded into the back of two pickups. Toriana stayed closely behind Lisa and loaded up with her. She looked around and saw the three women from the night before in the truck as well. *This must be my new group*, she concluded. She rested herself up against the side of the truck and took hold of it to prepare for an uncertain ride. She felt eyes on her and look back toward the front of the truck to see Daniel's smirk, once again trained on her, as he got into the driver's seat.

She heard Arlene giggle like a schoolgirl. Maggie, who was seated next to Arlene, elbowed her in the ribs. Maggie then asked Lisa, "Already, huh?" Lisa didn't answer.

Toriana gave Maggie a confused look to which Maggie responded, "Girl, I know you've spent your life stuffing dead deer but you gotta know when someone wants in your pants."

Lisa chimed in, "That asshole wants in everyone's pants...for a minute...until he gets it. Whatever."

With that, the conversation ended, with much tension left to linger.

Arlene then nervously asked, "So, what do you all think we are doing today?"

Toriana nearly repeated the question, "Yeah, what the hell *are* we doing?"

"Well, it looks like we are headed toward the pastures, so we are probably going to be doing fence work until dark," April answered.

There was a nearly unanimous groan. After a short trek down several gravel paths, the truck stopped in front of a damaged barbed wire fence. It appeared as if April had been right. The passengers began to dismount, beginning with the women in the back and then Daniel. He gave a series of short, gruff orders on the day's task and got back into the truck and drove about a hundred yards away.

Toriana had not heard the instructions. Truthfully, she found it hard to pay attention at all when he spoke. Almost mechanically, the huntresses began to grab tools that were unloaded from the truck and get to work on the fence. They went on in the same robotic fashion for hours and Toriana found it difficult to keep up. She had never repaired a fence, much less had she done so as a mechanism on an assembly line. The women rarely spoke. It was as if they communicated telekinetically.

Everyone's work ethic was interrupted by Daniel's shouting upon his return. Again, working on autopilot, the women herded toward the truck. They filed past an ice chest filled with meat and each took a portion, along with several bottles of water. They found spots on the ground and sat in their respective groups. Toriana, predictably, found her seat next to Lisa.

Lisa took a sloppy bite of her lunch and turned to Toriana, asking, "How ya hanging in there?"

Toriana raised her eyebrows, surprised at the question.

"That's about what I figured," Lisa said. "Don't worry about it, girly, it'll get better tonight."

Toriana nodded, confused. She looked up to Daniel's approaching shadow. He looked down at her and smiled a sly, evil grin.

"Has your mood improved any princess?"

Toriana quickly replied, "Naw, not quite yet. Is there something you can do about that?"

Daniel was rendered speechless. He only sounded a haughty chuckle and walked away, knowing he had been bested. The other women looked at Toriana queerly and she felt the heat of a blush pass over her cheeks. She had successfully tested the waters and found them quite agreeable.

In the following hours, what seemed like countless miles of fence had been patched and the women were loaded back into the truck beds.

"What now?" Toriana asked her companions.

Maggie asked, "Oh, do you mean after you blow Daniel?"

Everyone laughed but Toriana and Arlene. Arlene was clasping her hands over her ears to avoid any more crudeness and Toriana was stuttering trying to find a response. She couldn't figure out if it was an ill intended jab or a playful poke. Finding no reasonable conclusion, she joined into the laughter.

After recovering from her belly laugh, Lisa answered, "We are going back to the house to get ready for the hunt."

Toriana's was intrigued but she refrained from asking any further questions. After being dropped off at the house, the women split off into their respective rooms. Toriana watched from the hallway as they emerged, one by one, fully naked and in varying states of shift. She ducked into her doorway to strip down.

She was excited and confused. She closed her eyes and felt the pressure fill her thighs as they began to stiffen and swell. She took several short breaths as her ribs pulled apart to accommodate her growing lungs. The weight of her torso caused her to double over, but she felt her upper half slowly rising from the floor as they were supported by lengthening arms. She had not stopped the shift. She joined the women fully transformed.

With a quick shot of the eyes, she was beckoned forward. She found her place in the file as the pack lunged into the night, seeking a kill. Every wolf moved fluidly, in a dance rehearsed many times. Their efficiency and ruthlessness impressed Toriana. They moved through the forest silently, leaving no hint to the surrounding wildlife that they had come to seek and destroy. Each animal was taken back to the main house as it was executed. There it would be distributed.

As the night drew to a close, the huntresses picked off four more deer as their own reward. The women returned to the house and fatted themselves on a fresh kill. Toriana was blood drunk. She felt more powerful than she had in years. After the kills and after the feasts, the beasts cleaned themselves and prepared to return to human form.

Toriana remained, lingering on the her indulgences, and allowed her body to shrink in its own time. She was standing in a daze, naked and bloody when Lisa returned. Lisa, not speaking, exited the room and returned with a wet towel. She began to clean Toriana and stroke her skin. Toriana lowered herself to the floor in exhaustion and pure relaxation. Lisa remained beside her as she stared at the ceiling. Toriana's legs began to ache as she became more alert. She fidgeted with them until Lisa repositioned herself at Toriana's feet to caress out the tension.

"Its been a while since you shifted, hasn't it?" Lisa asked.

Toriana only nodded in affirmation. She then struggled to a seated position and looked wildly at her caregiver.

She asked, abruptly, "This is what we are made for, isn't it?"

Lisa returned her question with a shake of her head. Toriana continued to ramble for some time about how far their kind had gotten from their true nature, ending with "I'm going to fix this." Lisa looked at her with bewilderment, then chuckled and moved to stand up.

Toriana grabbed her wrist and with wildness that Lisa had seldom seen, said "No, please stay with me for a while and promise me that, no matter what, you will trust me."

Lisa returned to the floor and curled up next to her companion. She whispered in her ear "I trust you." Toriana slept soundly on the floor, cradled by her confused confidant.

Toriana's eyes opened to Daniel standing over her. On his face was a crude smile as he surveyed her naked body. It was morning. A morning for which Toriana was ill prepared. Lisa had left her at some point during the night but left behind a blanket, which Toriana now struggled to hide beneath. It was more a reflex to the shock than an act of modesty, for she had already made up her mind about Daniel.

"Rough night, princess?" Daniel asked, to which Toriana replied brazenly.

"Not as rough as I would have liked."

She could hear the others milling around in the bathroom. She shot to her feet, inches from Daniel, and turned away from him to expose her bare back. She could feel his eyes following as she sauntered to the showers. With no patience for the line in front of her, she walked directly into the shower area and into the stall with another woman. The woman yelped in shock amid gasps and peels of laughter from outside. Toriana rinsed off quickly and left walking right back by Daniel on her way to her room.

She quickly changed and returned to the main room just in time to file in with the rest of the huntresses. This time it was off to tend to the barns. It was back breaking and stinking work. Toriana worked slowly but diligently, taking special care to position herself directly in Daniel's line of sight. She would bend and stretch and flash looks in his direction. She did it coyly, as if begging to not be noticed.

When lunch break came, she feigned exhaustion. She huffed, panted, and fanned herself in such a way that any antebellum belle would be proud. Daniel took the bait. He pulled her to the side with the kind of concern that can only originate in the loins.

"You aren't going to pass out on me, are you?" he asked.

Toriana replied, "If I was going to pass out, I can think of worse places than on you."

"I'm serious, Tori, are you okay?" he asked.

Toriana took a second and stared at the ground, then brought up her eyes to meet his and said, "I think I might need to go lay down."

Daniel called out to the other men in the group that he would be heading back to the house for a minute. Toriana could feel the eyes of the other women upon her as she followed him to his pickup and lowered the tailgate to get inside. He stopped her.

"No, I think you should sit up front, so I can keep an eye on you" he said. Toriana gladly obliged.

Once back at the house, Toriana opened the truck door and moved to get out. She let her legs give way just in time for Daniel to catch her. The back of her hand came up to meet her face and her eyes rolled dizzily. Daniel easily pulled her back to her feet and wordlessly walked her inside.

Reaching the main foyer Daniel asked, "Do you want to lay down in your room or here?"

Toriana thought for a moment before coming to the answer.

"I think if I took a shower I would feel a bit better."

Daniel walked her to the bath area, unsure of his responsibility in this shower business. He sat her down on a chair that was positioned near the showers and carefully removed her boots. She thanked him profusely. Once her boots were off, he stood and spoke.

"I'm guessing you will want to take care of the rest."

Toriana panted, "Would you be willing to hold me up in the shower? I'd hate to pass out and hit my head."

Daniel nodded nervously. She reached out for his hand. As he pulled her to her feet, she reached through his arm to unbutton his pants.

"Wha...what are you doing?" he asked.

"Were you planning on getting your clothes soaked?" she asked in reply.

With his fly fully undone, Daniel steadied Toriana by putting his arm around her waist and began to pull her shirt off with his free hand. Now topless, Toriana pressed her body against his as she pressed down on the waistband of his pants until the dropped to the floor. She then ran her hands up his back, pushing his shirt up. This cued him to pull it the rest of the way off, putting them skin-to-skin.

Feeling her heat, Daniel pressed his mouth to hers and parted her lips with his tongue. His arm was around her waist and his free hand pressed against the back of her head, interweaving his fingers through her hair. He backed up clumsily until he reached the shower stall, where he turned the knob. Water sprayed over their bodies, knocking down sweat and inhibitions.

Toriana kept her eyes closed as they exchanged passionate kisses to mouth, neck, and body. However much a ploy this act was, she took some pleasure in it. Daniel turned her to face the wall of the shower and softly bit her neck. The pressure of his teeth brought a very real weakness in her legs.

Daniel, thinking she was experiencing symptoms of her "illness", stopped for a moment and asked, "Are you okay?"

It was an act of very real concern that almost made Toriana regret manipulating him. Pushing her guilt aside, she grabbed his hand and pulled it to her flower, moaning, "Don't stop."

He sped up his approach, pushing inside of her quickly. He had to brace himself against the wall, for it was his legs that weakened at feeling her. He rested his forehead on the top of her head as he pressed evenly and steadily. He took his time, relishing every thrust. As he neared climax, he wrapped his arms around her tightly and moved her on him as he moved in her. Toriana was now screaming and struggling to catch her breath as she too was nearly there. The sound of her exploding set his own detonation in motion. He pushed hard twice more. Holding on to her for dear life, he bent forward and rested his head on her shoulder. Toriana smiled: the trap was now firmly snapped into place.

They finished their shower together and walked to Toriana's room, dripping a path of water. Daniel gathered his clothes on his way out. Once inside her room, Toriana tossed a towel to Daniel and took one to dry herself.

As they redressed, Daniel said, "We both know you don't belong here."

Toriana responded, "I don't think any of us do, so why do I, particularly, not belong here?"

"Because you are smart and have a lot more going for you than any of the others. I honestly figured your dad would be here to get you by now," Daniel answered.

Toriana only shrugged and tackled him onto the bed. She straddled him and kissed him playfully. Daniel returned her affections and, coming up for air, joked, "I guess this means I'm welcome back?"

Toriana shrugged again. Daniel reversed their positions and kissed her on the cheek. He pushed her dripping hair away from her face and said, "I'd better go before everyone starts wondering what's going on. All hell would break loose if this got out."

"I'm sure it would," she said.

With that simple fact understood, Daniel returned to work.

Toriana took his leaving as an opportunity to catch a short nap before the night's hunt. It seemed like mere minutes later when she heard the sound of huntresses stampeding through the foyer. Her door unceremoniously burst open. Lisa slammed the door behind her.

"What the fuck, girl?"

"What?" Toriana asked, momentarily playing stupid.

"I would ask if you are okay but I'm smarter than ol' Danny boy and I know you faked that shit today." Lisa was growing impatient. Toriana involuntarily cracked a smile.

"You dirty bitch, you did him, didn't you?" Lisa exclaimed in a tone that indicated she was not pleased. Without giving Toriana a chance to answer, she went into a diatribe.

"I don't know what you think you have going but slutting-out isn't going to get you far with him. You aren't the first, you won't be the..."

"Lisa"

"Last. Not to mention the fact that you have some serious damage control..."

"Lisa"

"To do with the rest of the girls now and I'm sorry there is nothing I can do to help..."

"LISA" Toriana finally screamed.

Lisa matched her tone, asking, "What?"

Toriana walked to the door and cracked it open to check if anyone was eavesdropping. Confident that it was clear, she asked Lisa to sit down. Lisa threw her hands up in defeat and plopped down on the bed. Toriana began to explain.

"First off, I don't care what is being said out there, so do not start on me about damage control. This is a hell of a lot more complicated than what you think and I need you to make a decision right now whether you trust me or not."

Lisa, just as the night before, was very confused. She saw a steely hardness in Toriana's eyes that she had never seen in another. Lisa's face lost all sign of arrogance. She looked up at

Toriana and said, "Okay, I trust you. I don't know what you are doing but get after it I guess. What do you need from me?"

"Just keep the lynch mob as calm as you can for a little while." Toriana said.

With that Lisa rose to her feet and moved for the door, turning to Toriana as she walked out, saying, "You better shift out for the hunt." This sealed a silent pact between the women.

Toriana could see betrayal even in the shifted faces of the other huntresses as she found her place in formation. She was pushed to the back of the hunting force and found herself sitting alone during the feast. She ate little, shifting back early, re-showering, and retiring to her room.

This routine continued for the following few nights. Daniel's faint knocks at her window in the middle of the night became part of her routine as well. The visits first brought fierce and thrilling carnal pleasures but began to taper into long nights of kissing and talking. This could have easily became a feeling of forbidden romance, if not for Toriana's true intent.

One night, after several hours of sweaty writhing, Daniel asked, "Can you get away tomorrow?"

Toriana shot him a puzzled look. Daniel continued.

"There is a bonfire tomorrow night. It's a relationship building function with us and the Kleines. I'd like to take you as my date."

Toriana, still more confused than anything, asked, "Are you sure that's a good idea?"

The look on Daniel's face indicated that he did not know the answer to the question but he confessed, "I care about you, Tori. I don't want this to end when you go home."

Toriana was pleased to hear this but not in the love-struck way she might be expected to. However, the smile she gave Daniel looked the same either way. Toriana threw her arms around him and accepted the invitation, but on one condition.

"I will only go if some of the other girls are allowed to come with me."

Daniel bit his bottom lip but found that he could not deny Toriana's pleading eyes.

"Okay, but just a few. And please not Amber," Daniel said and they both burst into laughter.

Moments later Daniel dressed and crept back out of the door. Once he was fully gone, Toriana rushed to Lisa's room, jumped into bed with her and shook her awake.

Lisa groggily asked "What, are you off your meds?"

Without acknowledging the question, Toriana burst.

"Tell Maggie, April, and Arlene that we are all skipping the hunt tomorrow night."

"What?" Lisa asked. Toriana explained.

"Daniel is taking us to a bonfire party tomorrow night. It's a diplomatic thing with the Krams and Kleine heavy hitters. Tell them they need to put on the charm where they can. I'll see you in the morning."

With that Toriana disappeared back out of the door and went to bed. Lisa sat up for a minute, trying to understand the request, before giving up and returning to her sleep.

As she worked the next day, Toriana suddenly felt herself being pulled into a clump of trees. Before her were her companions of choice, looking at her as if she had a horn growing out of her head. Maggie spoke first.

"What, again, are we doing tonight?"

Toriana tried to play it down, as best as she could.

"It is just a little get together that I was able to get a few invites for."

April wasn't satisfied.

"Bullshit, Tori. What's this diplomatic charm thing all about?"

"Yes, it's an inter-pack bon fire and I need all of you to make yourselves adorable. Except April. I just need you to enjoy yourself and play wing man, wing woman, whatever."

April again demanded further information.

"But why?"

Toriana was frustrated.

"Don't worry about the why. Just have fun, drink, flirt, play horseshoes and let me worry about the why."

With that she walked off. That was the last time she spoke to them until returning to the house that evening. Things went as it was customary for them to go. The remaining huntresses prepared for the hunt, leaving behind Toriana and her rogues. The women dressed as well as they could, considering their limited options. Most had long ago abandoned all notions of feminine grace and it showed. Daniel arrived and the rag-tag crew loaded in to the truck, but into the cab this time.

Toriana wedged herself into the middle of the front bench seat, between Daniel and Lisa. Daniel took her hand, full of pride, joyful to show off his prize. During the ride the three girls in the back whispered and snickered among themselves. It made Daniel a bit uncomfortable and he more than once tried, in his most friendly voice, to engage them in conversation but got no response. After several miles, the warm glow of a large fire peaked above the cedars. They rounded the wood line to find the good ol' boy club celebrating to their heart's content.

The patrons of the night's festivities were exclusively male, to April's disappointment. Toriana had expected it. The truck came to a rest and the women stepped out. Few noticed their arrival but as they neared the crowd, stares shifted in their direction. Fortunately the beer had been flowing for some hours and few protested. Suddenly, a tired looking older man rushed to them and took Arlene into his arms. Arlene began to sob, saying to him, "I'm much better, Daddy. I'm so much better."

The other women each reacted in her own way to this display. Some faces turned angry and others began to tear up. The two disappeared to the fringes of the crowd, where they remained for the duration of the night. The remaining members scattered, presumably wishing to either find or hide from their own family. Toriana had ignorantly overlooked the possibility of family reunions impeding her plan. She concluded that she would have to do this on her own.

She clutched Daniel's arm and whispered in his ear.

"I recall you wanted to show me off."

Daniel nodded, shaking off the shock of witnessing Arlene and her father. They walked into the thick of the crowd, saying hello's along the way.

The couple neared the nucleus of a tightly gathered bunch of men and made their way to greet Leo Kleine. Leo's congenial smile dropped in surprise when he realized the identity of the woman on Daniel's arm. Struggling to compose himself, Leo addressed Toriana first.

"Toriana" he said, "I wasn't expecting you. I see that you are getting along well."

With the last statement he eyed Daniel. Toriana answered defiantly.

"Better than expected, Leo."

Leo placed his hand on the young man next to him. This got the young man's attention and he turned to face Toriana.

Leo said, "You may not remember my son, Matthew. Matthew, this is Toriana Wittlich."

Matthew stuck out his hand and replied, "Oh, yes, I remember. How are you doing, with...you know...everything?"

Everyone within earshot cringed at Matthew's bold question. Toriana smiled at him to ease his embarrassment, indicating both forgiveness and wellness. Immediately the subject changed to pack affairs, with Leo and Daniel pretending not to size each other up. Toriana acted the trophy girl and remained silent but took the opportunity to coyly grin at Matthew at every available moment. Matthew acted as if he had not seen her at first but after several attempts, Toriana got his eyes to linger.

Matthew was known widely as a shy and naive young man. The chatter among pack leaders had long been that Leo was hesitant to pass the torch to Matthew, fearing that he lacked the wherewithal to lead. Toriana turned to Daniel and told him that she was going to go and check on the rest of the girls. Daniel kissed her cheek and watched her walk away. He was totally smitten. Toriana wandered the edge of the darkness until she found a somewhat hidden nook to lie in wait.

Within moments, Matthew found her. He had easily slipped away as his father and Daniel entrenched themselves in politics. Sensing her scent as he passed by, Matthew halted and turned to Toriana. He began nervously.

"I was looking for you. I wanted to apologize for bringing up your situation. I'm really sorry. It was dumb."

Toriana waved her hand in front of her face and sucked on her bottom lip.

"Its okay, I'm fine," she said, before feigning some sobs.

Matthew walked closer to her and she leapt into his arms, hiding her face. She needed to disguise the lack of tears. She heaved heavily and rubbed her eyes to get them to water. Matthew held her closely and shushed her kindly, continuing to apologize. As Toriana pulled back, she ran her hands down her face, spreading the few tears she could produce.

Matthew, grasping for a way to comfort her, asked, "Do you miss your dad?"

Toriana continued to sniffle, answering, "It's just everything. You don't know what its like in that house. Whoring myself out to Daniel is the only way to survive. They are all out to break me."

Matthew, astounded at her answer, stuttered, "You mean you aren't...you don't..you.."

Toriana cut him off, feigning outrage.

"Hell no. How could I want to be with a monster like him? He's the one who keeps us prisoner, all of us." Toriana played on huntress lore.

Matthew reached out to hug her again and she pushed him away, begging, "Oh, god, you can't tell him. Please no. He'll kill us. Please. You can't tell anyone!"

Matthew gave his word and added, "I want to help you. I want to help all of you. Tell me how."

Toriana involuntarily kissed him. She felt a delightfully growing bulge below his belt as she put the whole of her body against his. Parting from him, she ran his hand across the side of his face and told him, "I have to go before he gets suspicious. I'll meet you behind the huntress house at 1 am tomorrow night. Please tell me you will come for me."

Matthew promised. He had no idea what he had gotten himself into.

*****

Watching him for a few moments as he trotted away, Toriana marveled at the depths to which she had decided to go. She wasn't altogether sure of her plan. Would she be able to pull it off? And if so, with what consequences?

She only knew for sure, in that moment, that she must ready herself for whatever may come. The first step was to cover her tracks. She remembered Daniel. She had to get back to him before he came looking for her. She went looking for her partners in crime, finding one of them sooner than expected.

Stumbling clumsily from the wood line just a few feet away was Maggie. She looked disheveled and obviously in better spirits than when she arrived. She glanced over to notice Toriana and flashed a coy smile as she walked over. Toriana only shook her head and commented.

"I'm not even going to ask. Where are the rest of the girls?"

"I don't know. I've been a little tied up", she replied.

Toriana tilted her head to one side in mock disgust. Maggie again grinned then followed Toriana's lead to walk toward, the crowd only to find that it had thinned significantly. The party had begun to wind to a halt without them having noticed.

Now feeling a rush of panic, she headed toward where they had parked the truck. As she neared it, she could make out a gaggle of figures surrounding it. Daniel's voice shattered the low hum of people leaving.

"Looks like you managed to round up the last of them."

Toriana exaggerated an affirmative nod so that it could be

recognized. Maggie whispered from the side of mostly closed mouth, "What were you doing in the woods anyway?"

Toriana hummed back, "Scouting, I'll explain later."

As they stepped closer to the truck, Toriana could see an odd look spreading across Daniel's face. It was if he recognized something but could not place it. Bringing Toriana in for a warm kiss, he pulled back quickly. His expression returned to suspicion but this time more intensely. Toriana panicked inside but managed a flirtatious, "What, baby?"

"I smell something on your. Where have you been?" he asked.

Maggie stepped in.

"I was a little weak in the knees after a little adventure in the woods. I leaned on her. That's one hell of a good time you smell."

Daniel's face turned to contempt, with no attempt to mask it. With that, they loaded themselves in the truck.

Once back at the house, the girls quickly unloaded, eager to exchange stories. Toriana attempted to follow them into the house, but was quickly stopped by Daniel.

"I guess now there is no need for me to sneak in to spend the night" he said.

Toriana knew she had to establish some distance if she was to execute the next phase of her plan. She had run out of time to come up with an excuse.

"I've been thinking about that," she started, "I think its time to cool down a bit. Everyone else at the party made it no secret that they didn't approve."

Daniel rushed to interject, "But I don't care about that!"

Toriana stopped him short.

"You have a promising future, Daniel, you need to protect it. I'm not saying its over. I'm just saying that I care too much about you to allow this to jeopardize your position in the hoard. We just have to give them a minute to get accustomed to the idea...that's all."

Daniel looked at her in wonder.

"I admire this in you. Just promise me its not over. Please."

Toriana took his face in her hands and whispered, "I promise."

He took her hand and kissed it, gave a warm smile and walked away. Toriana turned toward the house, barely breathing as she walked inside. Once behind the safety of the front door, she heavily exhaled, thankful for her ploy having worked. Lisa appeared seemingly out of nowhere.

With no regard for Toriana's obviously shaken demeanor she said, "Well, you sneaky little bitch. This is where you should probably put the pieces together for me."

Toriana begrudgingly agreed, requesting that Lisa gather her remaining conspirators in her room. More quickly than she expected, Toriana's quarters were besieged by curious young women. However, one was missing.

Toriana asked the room, "Where is Arlene?"

April was the first to answer.

"You must really have it bad for Daniel to not have noticed she wasn't in the truck on the way home. Her family kept her. Lucky bitch."

Toriana was relieved. She had often worried about Arlene's tenacity and ability to withstand the pressure that was sure to befall her band of dissenters. Without addressing this relief aloud, she began by correcting April.

"I don't have it bad for anyone. Look, there are things in the works right now and I need all of you to decide whether you are going to be a part of it or not. If not, you need to leave right now."

No one so much as blinked. Toriana took a breath and let it out.

"I'm going to start a war."

The girls were stunned into deafening silence at the statement. Toriana continued.

"Daniel is a pawn. He's in love with me and, pretty soon, Matthew Klein is going to be in love with me too. Matthew already knows about Daniel but when Daniel finds out about Matthew, all hell is going to break loose. I'm hoping that, in the confusion, we can get out of here."

She waited for a response but received none. In the silence, she issued a cryptic statement

"If the hell comes down on me and y'all are involved in all this, it's going to come down on you too."

Lisa asked the question on everyone's lips.

"So what's the plan after our grand exit?"

Toriana answered, "It is going to take some time to pull it all together."

Lisa, although dissatisfied, dropped the subject for the moment, not wanting to force Toriana into admitting that she hadn't thought that far ahead. Toriana had a plan, however, she was unsure of the loyalties in the room and had no intentions of revealing it. Lisa, as she had promised, trusted her friend.

The next day at work, Toriana noticed Daniel's longing glances but all but ignored them. She kept her mind on what was to come that night when Matthew arrived. As huntresses toiled away at digging a series of irrigation ditches, Daniel called Toriana over and loudly proclaimed that he needed her to remove a rock from their intended path. When she arrived, she noticed a small stone with the words "I love you" written in the dirt around it. She looked up at him and mouthed "you too" then quickly removed the rock and swept over the message with her boot.

She was surprised at how deeply his infatuation for her had implanted itself into his mind. *Poor dumb bastard*, she thought. Wrapping up the day's work, the women got into the truck to head home. Toriana returned to her position in the bed of the pickup. Nothing appeared out of the ordinary and no one seemed to take notice of Toriana's clandestine activities until they returned to the house.

Within moments of walking through the door, Toriana found herself surrounded by a group of young women. Amber, acting as ringleader, asked, "So Whoriana, you gonna skip out of the hunt again?"

Toriana had dreaded this moment but expected it. All she could manage to reply was, "You don't have a clue what you are talking about, so get the hell out of my way" as she pushed thought the crowd.

Amber chased after her, taunting and demanding answers. Weeks worth of rage bubbled, inching their way to the surface as Toriana halted midway down the hall. Swiftly, she turned and, in a single movement, took Amber around the throat and lifted her off the ground against a wall. She squeezed harder as Amber struggled through her own terror to shift. Amber's vision became tunneled as she could feel herself loosing consciousness and, in an act of self-preservation, gave up. Toriana felt the muscled around Amber's neck soften and lowered her to the ground. With her hand still firmly in place around Amber's neck, Toriana positioned her face inches from Amber's and in barley more than a whisper said, "Leave me the fuck alone." Confident from Amber's wide eyes that she had gotten the message, Toriana released her grip and went to her room slamming the door behind her.

Toriana's heart rate continued to race as she plopped down on her bed. Aside from the expected schoolyard scuffles, she had never had to show such an act of aggression against one of her own. Violence between werewolves was strongly discouraged and perhaps the strongest of social taboos. The fear was that once wolves began to reap destruction on each other, the hoard would collapse so it was avoided when at all possible. Toriana, however, felt a deep rush inside of her unlike anything she had ever felt. Surprisingly, she felt no guilt or fear of reprisal. She had shown her strength against another wolf and it had worked.

She did skip the hunt that night. She, instead, sat on the edge of her bed, intently watching a beat up clock that she was sure predated her presence on earth. It slowly ticked toward 1 am.. She carefully rehearsed, taking care to exploit every vulnerability Matthew could possibly have. As the hour drew close, she knew that she had reached a point from which she could never return. She would secure her fate in one fell swoop tonight.

She quietly moved through the house, reaching the back door. She walked out to await Matthew's arrival. Within moments, and far earlier than expected, there was a rustling in the leaves. Toriana was surprised. She asked out loud.

"Where is your truck? Did you walk here?"

He answered that he had parked a half-mile down the road and walked the rest of the way. He didn't want to put Toriana in danger by being detected. Toriana took the opportunity to lavish praise upon Matthew.

"You are so kind and thoughtful" she cooed, "I cannot begin to thank you enough for coming here."

Matthew was visibly flattered, sticking his hands in his pockets and kicking at the leaves in his shyness. Toriana drew closer to him, placing her hand on his work-toned arm and kissing him on the cheek.

Matthew turned to her and asked, "What can I do to help you?"

Just as rehearsed, Toriana answered.

"I'm afraid there is little you can do. I just...what I really need is someone to lean on. I need someone to care for me through this. I'm so terribly lonely." She began to cry a bit.

Matthew, as expected, wrapped his arms around her to shush her. He began to whisper to her.

"I can do that. I'll come every night if I have to."

Toriana lifted her head and kissed him. She wanted to seal the deal. She pushed her tongue into his mouth deeply, lightly stroking his tongue with hers. She dragged her fingers down his chest until she reached his belt. She ran them up again, this time under his shirt. She reached around his back, sinking her nails gently into the sensitive skin as she pressed her body against his. She felt the firmness in his groin pressing into her body and worked her hand down to place it in her grasp. She massaged him through his jeans while she kissed his neck.

Matthew breathed heavily and quickly, pulsating beneath her touch. She brought her mouth to his ear and instructed him to lay down. He gladly obeyed. She followed him to the ground and unbuttoned his blue jeans, pulling away any barriers between her and her prize. She wiggled free of her pajama pants, revealing glistening bare skin and positioned herself on top of him. Her knees clinched tightly at his waist and as she lowered herself onto him.

Finding its mark quickly, his manhood filled her, bringing them both to a moan. She made a wave of her body as she used her weight to feel every inch of him. Pulling back from each stroke, she almost allowed their bodies to separate but stopped just short, pushing him back inside. The pace quickened, causing her to sink her heels into his legs for leverage. She wasn't screaming - she didn't have the breath too.

Wetness rushed onto him as she reached her peak and kept going to give him his. She knew he was close when she felt him swell still more inside of her and saw him close his eyes. Once more he plunged into her and, with that, he quivered into ecstasy. Toriana stopped, leaving him inside her while she bent down to kiss him lightly on the lips. She smiled in a way that made him believe she was satisfied. Indeed, she was far more physically satisfied than expected but he was witnessing a look of accomplishment that went far deeper than he could have imagined.

She remained on him, kissing his face and smiling, until she heard a noise for which she could not account. She looked up and peered through the darkness. There, not more than 10 feet away, stood Daniel. She jumped up from her position but could not form words.

In a streak of pure rage, Daniel rushed to Matthew and pulled him from the ground. Toriana rushed to her clothes to get dressed and ran between them, using her strength to push both men to the ground. With this, Daniel refocused her anger at Toriana.

"What the hell is this?"

Matthew didn't give her an opportunity to answer. Filling his knight in shining armor role perfectly, he shouted, "This is the end of your bullshit, Daniel. You and your family are not going to do this to these women anymore."

Daniel was clearly shocked. What came from him next was a series of profanities and threats further confused by Matthew's overlapping replies. Toriana out-shouted them both, demanding that they leave. By now, the huntresses were gathering at the windows trying to figure out what had happened. Daniel issued one last threat, this time to Toriana.

"You want to act like one of these whores, you can be treated like one. You have no idea how bad it can get."

With that he retreated, spinning gravel beneath his truck tires as he sped away. Matthew took Toriana's hand and began to promise that nothing would happen to her. She could barely hear him over the sound of her mind at work. This was not how this was to happen. It was too quick. Real tears of fear gathered on his face this time. Matthew told her to just stay put, promising, "I'm going to go take care of this." The war had started.

Toriana knew that she had started this. She had single-handedly put the wheels in motion that brought this moment. She, however, was ill prepared for the expediency with which it happened. She stood alone, half naked and heart racing. She knew Daniel and Matthew were but miles from the armies that they would undoubtedly assemble.

Toriana was left with no other option than to mobilize her own in kind. She suddenly regretted her having so closely guarded her intentions. She should have prepared the other women better. They were, as of this moment, unknowingly thrust into civil war and it was Toriana's responsibility to tell them.

She burst through the back door shouting as loudly as she could. She could not simply call out to them. She had made too many enemies for that. She had to create such a commotion as to coax them from their beds. She ran to the parlor and began overturning furniture and banging against the walls. As expected, the women emerged from the now nonexistent security of their beds. Some donned expressions of confused curiosity with others clearly advertising anger and contempt.

"We've got a major problem," she announced. "The Krams and Klein families are about to break into civil war."

She heard gasps from the crowd.

"Within the hour, this place is going to be ground zero. You've all got an option. You can follow me out of here and give yourselves a chance at freedom or you can stay and become a victim to whatever happens."

One young woman stepped forward of the crowd and, voice wavering, asked, "What are you talking about? What happened?"

Toriana, sensing her fear, took her hand and softly said, "I wish there was time to explain it all. But there's not. Right now you have to decide if this place is all there is for you."

Toriana felt a deep sense of guilt for pulling these women into a sequence of events for which they were not prepared. She only hoped that some ember of the fire that had been stomped out in them could reignite them into the fight. Lisa turned to the crowd and shouted, "I personally don't care if you stay or if you go with us, but if you are going, you had better start packing your shit, because we aren't waiting around much longer. Just pack light."

Lisa had a way of communicating a sense of urgency.

The parlor electrified as young women disbursed. Toriana

could not be sure how many would follow. She turned her attention to her personal preparations. She went to her room and gathered her single bag and removed from it any non-essential items. All that remained were her cherished mementos. Lisa and Maggie met her at the hall as she was leaving her room for the last time.

"Okay what's the plan" Lisa asked.

Toriana asked in return, "You know these woods, right, Lisa?"

Lisa nodded in affirmation.

"Maggie, I need you to get back to the parlor and tell everyone that's going that they need to shift and meet in front of the house in 5 minutes. Lisa, you are going to lead us out to the main roads. After that we will trace the wood line to my house."

The last statement startled Lisa and she asked, "Isn't that the first place they will look for us?"

"Probably, but getting a base will buy us some time for me to get reinforcements," Toriana answered.

Lisa, trusting her friend just as she was asked, only nodded and walked away. When Toriana got outside, she got first glimpse of her band of confederates. They were smaller in number than expected but there was no time to dwell on inadequacies. They took flight behind Lisa, maintaining hunt formation until they approached the main road. Toriana stepped cautiously out front, listening closely for any sign of approaching wolves.

They bounded across the road in pairs, quietly and skillfully and traced along it making their way to Toriana's little cottage. When they arrived, Toriana motioned for the huntresses to fan out and confirm that they were, in fact, alone. Once the area was cleared, Toriana alone approached the door, finding it locked. She ripped it from the hinges. Inside, she found her home remarkably little different than when she left it. Her truck was in the driveway and keys on the table. The sheets were still ruffled from her last night's sleep there. Confident that they had found their secure base, she again motioned pack forward.

The women gathered, still shifted, into the front room of the cottage, where Toriana gave the next set of directives.

"I need four volunteers to stay in shift and post up at the corners of the house and one more to stand guard at the front door. Whoever stays at the front door will be responsible for alerting the rest of us if there is any trouble, as well as rotating out the guards so everyone gets to eat and rest."

Four silently exited the room and took up positions outside as Lisa manned the door.

The confused and tired women milled about in the front room as Toriana walked into the bedroom. She whispered a thank you to herself for having kept a landline phone at house despite having little need for it. She picked up the receiver and dialed the only outside ally she could have hoped to have. The phone rang multiple time, Toriana making terse please for an answer between them.

Eventually, Evan picked up. He voice was cautious and concerned. He had heard of what had become of Toriana and could hardly understand why he was suddenly receiving a call from her. Once he heard her voice on the line, his caution faded into panicked questions.

"Tori what happened? Are you okay? What did they do to you there? Did they already let you go?"

Toriana cut him off.

"I'm in trouble Evan. I need your help. Can you please just come here? I'll explain everything."

He answered that he would come immediately. Toriana hung up the phone and rushed to Lisa to let her know they were expecting welcome company. She described Evan and his vehicle to Lisa so that she could relay it to the guard force outside. While she waited, she pulled pounds of meat from the freezer to thaw. She didn't know how long they would be in one place, but she knew the troops needed to be fed.

The wait for Evan's arrival was short. Lisa escorted him to Toriana so that his identity could be verified. There was no need for words as Toriana leaped into his arms. The gravity of the situation suddenly befell her and she dissolved into tears.

"I'm so sorry. I'm so damn sorry for everything I did to you," she sobbed.

Evan hushed her, gathering her shoulders in his hands.

"Judging from the army you've recruited, there is much more going on than anything you did to me. Tell me what is happening," he said.

There was no judgment in his voice, only tenderness that Toriana had so sorely missed. Toriana took his hand and led him into the bedroom. Once there, she began the story.

"I've done unforgivable things, Evan. The only explanation I can offer you is that it was what I had to do."

Evan nodded as if to say he was ready to hear what she was about to say. Toriana recounted the events as calmly as she could, everything from Lisa's scars to her own sexual exploitation of the Krams and Klein men. She felt horribly ashamed.

Evan sighed heavily and said, "You didn't ask me here to confess your sins. You need my help. What am I doing?"

He squeezed her hand tightly, punctuating his question with forgiveness. Toriana, gathering herself and wiping away the last remnants of tears, laid out the next phase of her plan.

"I need an emergency council meeting. Do you think your father would be open to making that happen?"

"I'm sure he would" Evan said. "How much does he need to know?"

"Everything," Toriana answered. "I need for him to tell Daddy and the Bedburgs that he heard of the uproar with the Krams and Klein families and that a large group of huntresses are on the loose. There needs to be an immediate meeting to resolve the issue. That is all they need to know."

"When should this meeting happen?" Evan asked.

"Tonight. Do you think he will support us?" Toriana asked.

Evan smiled mischievously.

"When he hears about what's been done to these girls, hell yes."

Toriana wrapped Evan in a warm embrace and kissed his cheek.

She whispered, "Thank you".

For the first time, she felt an odd sense of safety. Evan rose from the bed, with her hand still in his.

"I'd better go get the ball rolling. If you need me, call me. I'll call you as soon as I know something." He knelt down to kiss her forehead and pleaded, "Please be safe for me." With that he left.

Toriana exited the bedroom. She went to Lisa and asked how everyone was holding up. It was now after daybreak and fatigue was clearly setting in. Lisa answered that she had already rotated the guards out. Toriana told Lisa to get some sleep, that she would take the door. Lisa, in the typical way, refused to leave her post.

Toriana went to the kitchen and started distributing still partially frozen chunks of meat, imploring each girl to get some sleep after they had eaten. A short time later, the house fell quiet but for the soft snores of sleeping women. They were scattered along the floor, the couches, and a few slumbered in Toriana's bed. She walked about placing rolled towels under the heads of those who had nothing else to cushion themselves and blankets over the huddled groups.

Every two hours, like clockwork, Lisa would awaken groups of four so that they could relieve the outside guards. Toriana was infinitely proud of these women. Though disposable misfits to their families, they were warriors in their own right. Toriana found a seat against the far wall of the main room, still within eyeshot of Lisa should she have trouble.

She dozed briefly but was startled awake by the ringing phone.

She picked up the receiver silently, letting whoever was on the other end be the first to speak.

"Its Evan. The meeting is on for 6 pm. My dad is pissed about what was done and your dad is losing his mind wondering where you are. Don't be surprised if he shows up there."

Toriana looked at the clock and realized that the meeting was only a few hours away. She knew that her father could show up at any minute.

"Shit" was her only reply.

"I'm coming to you," Evan said. "And I'm bringing some others from the pack. My father insisted."

Toriana replied, "Okay, just please hurry."

Without so much as a pause, Evan responded to her plea, promising he would hurry and saying, "Hang in there. I love you."

Toriana was shocked, not only at Evan's proclamation but that she responded without hesitation.

"I love you too."

However, there was no time to relish this moment. She quickly hung up the phone and went to Lisa.

"We are going to have some company," Toriana said.

Lisa, assuming the worst, asked, "Who and how many?"

Toriana told her, "Evan and some members of his pack are coming to help but there is one other problem. It's my father. He is not exactly welcome but I don't want him attacked. I want him escorted in, brought immediately to me, and closely guarded, for our protection and his."

Lisa was confused.

"What if he brings a posse with him, what then?"

Toriana felt the weight of this decision as she told Lisa, "Take care of the problem, but don't hurt my father."

Evan and his entourage arrived and he went directly to Toriana, this time without an escort. He kissed her and told her, "I brought enough men to stand guard at the door and outside. We can take care of that while you get everyone else ready for the meeting."

"Okay," Toriana replied and turned to tell Lisa what was happening.

Evan took her hand and said, "Whatever happens tonight, please don't....I can't lose you again."

She wrapped herself around him and said, "I'm not going anywhere."

With that, she went again to Lisa. She told her she could take a rest, the guard shift would be covered. However, she needed everyone gathered no later than 5:30 to be given an update on what was to happen next. She thanked her friend. By this time most of the women were awake and alert, a few of them flirting with the Fahrenholz men. Maggie, not surprisingly, led this activity.

An unexpected rumbling of tires on gravel got Toriana's attention. She wondered if the Krams and Klein men had already tired of fighting each other and made their move to seek her out. Seconds passed that seemed like hours until the source of the noise came into view. It was her father.

She should have been relieved but strangely her anxiety

climbed even higher. She shouted for Evan, who ran into the room and she asked him to intercept her father and bring him to her. She watched through he window as Dietrich exited the truck and practically ran inside, with Evan rushing to catch him. Dietrich immediately found his daughter, stretching out his arms and asking if she was okay.

Toriana denied him an embrace, instead holding her ground proudly.

"Oh, my child, what have you done?" he asked.

Her lips tightened together in a grimace, as if the very questions pierced her skin.

"Its what you have done. Everything that is happening is your doing," she exclaimed.

Lisa, hearing the shout, ran into the room and to Toriana's side. Toriana assured Lisa that everything was alright.

"We all have a meeting to attend at 6 pm. Tell the girls to be ready for a fight, if it comes to that."

Dietrich was shocked at hearing this. He had never imagined this kind of coldness from his little girl.

"What is it that you intend to accomplish?" he asked.

"Changes are coming, Daddy. You'll either move with them, or move against them, but I warn you, I have enough backing to put up one hell of a fight."

Dietrich did not want a fight. He had given so much of himself to prevent just this. Solemn in his defeat, he asked, "I suppose you hate me?"

Relaxing her face, Toriana said, "I don't hate you, Daddy. I hate what you've done and what you've allowed to happen for the sake of some flawed sense of civility. I won't allow it anymore. I don't want to make an enemy of you but if you do not fall on your sword, I won't have much of a choice."

In that moment Dietrich wanted nothing more than to find peace with his daughter, while somehow holding on to his dignity. He came to a compromise within himself and told his daughter, "I won't be a puppet. If you want the power to change things then you will also have the responsibility. You'll take over my council seat fully. I only hope that you will be as dutiful as you are relentless."

Toriana finally had what she had fought so hard for and took pride in her victory, but not in her father's defeat. She looked at him and asked, "Will you accompany me to the meeting?" He gracefully obliged.

As the hour of promise crept up, the atmosphere grew tense and anxious. These women had followed Toriana into an uncertain fate on limited information. She knew that she must address their fears. She rose her voice above the hum of the crowd.

"I know you all put a great deal of faith in me by following me out. Tonight, I plan on earning that faith. At this meeting, I plan on putting a stop the practice of throwing away women and letting the men who imprison them act with impunity. Talking may simply not be enough. I've already asked a great deal of you, I know. But now I must ask that all of you stand your ground no matter how threatening the night may turn to be. If our failure seems imminent, I would not look down on any of you for saving yourselves. And if that happens, please know that I am sorry. Here in a few minutes we are going to head out for the meeting. I need half of you to accompany me inside the council house and the rest to stay outside."

Silence filled the room. Everyone, including Dietrich and the Fahrenholz men, stared blank faced at Toriana. Sensing Toriana's anticipation, Evan joined her at the front of the group. He pledged that the Fahrenholz men would stand and fight beside them, no matter the cost. Being reassured that they were not alone in the fight seemed to encourage the women and they gave enthusiastic shouts, readying themselves for the potential battle. The newly formed pack left Toriana's cottage in a long convoy of pick up trucks. Each woman found herself in a seat opposed to the bed. This was something that Toriana took great pride in.

They arrived at the council house right on time. Toriana, seated next to Evan, scanned the parking lot for potential threats. The Klein and Krams representatives, as planned, had not been invited. Toriana had no idea what was going on with the two families, but worried deeply for the women left behind at the huntress lair. The convoy parked, one at a time, and offloaded its occupants. With the same efficiency that Toriana had witnessed while hunting with these women, half of them fanned out around the council house and the others followed her to the front door. Lisa, who chose to stay with those guarding the perimeter, gave Toriana a wink.

Toriana, the half the huntress pack, the Fahrenholz men, and Dietrich came through the door. Frank Fahrenholz smiled as the huntresses fanned out around the room and Toriana took her seat in Dietrich's chair. Clause Bedburg looked surprised, to say the least. He had not been prepared for this. He, however, did not immediately question it. Frank was the first to speak.

"Toriana, nice to see you back." he said.

Toriana flashed him a smile and replied, "Nice to be back, Frank."

Clause took this opportunity to get some clarity and asked, "It is good to see you but what are you doing back, and in your father's chair, no less?"

"Clause, I am in my father's chair because he has passed his position on to me. I am a full member of the council and, as such, I have some pieces of business that need to be attended to. As you may be aware, the Krams and Klein families are no doubt engaging in all out civil war by now. What you may not know is what brought the war about. Having been a Krams prisoner for the past several weeks, I am in a very good position to tell you. Do you see these women around you? These are former huntresses, and if you walk outside, you will see a number more of them. Each of these women was outcast by her family, abused, exploited, and enslaved. And they, gentlemen, are why our two problem families are at odds with each other as we speak."

Toriana paused to give this revelation time to sink in. Frank interrupted the moment, saying, "I have recently been informed of what goes on in that camp, what these men are doing. I won't stand for it, Clause, and you shouldn't either. Toriana, if you have a plan for putting a stop to this I would love to hear it."

Clause spoke up. "I don't like what I'm hearing but I'm more concerned with this war you are speaking up. It stands to expose us all. We have got to protect the hoard."

"Protect the hoard at the cost of what, Clause" Toriana asked. "Furthermore, how does letting two families continuously disgrace all that we are protect us and our kind? The Krams are the perpetrators and the Kleins are their enablers. They gain off of the backs of the huntresses, just as they gained off the backs of the Krams. I propose a resolution be passed at this meeting that demands that the Krams immediately shut down their slave operation and that both families come to a peace agreement along with land distribution within the next three days. They must also be forbidden from retaliating against the huntresses."

"How do you propose to enforce this resolution?" Clause asked.

"Tonight, after the resolution is passed, a meeting will be arranged with the Krams and Klein leadership. They will sign the resolution and make good on terms or they will be severed from the hoard. They will lose any sway in the council and any access to hoard resources. I'll be glad to hand deliver the resolution. I will, however, require reinforcements to my new pack members, should violence occur."

Clause began insisting that this action would never work but his words quickly became undecipherable beneath Frank's insistence that it would and must. Finally, Dietrich spoke.

"We have all made dangerously misguided decisions in our

efforts to protect this hoard. Mine, however, were the most appalling. The Krams and Klein families have been as a sword blade to this hoard. The harder we try to hold onto it, the more deeply it cuts us. In adopting this resolution, peace is not guaranteed but by failing to take action war is guaranteed."

Toriana felt a renewed sense of pride in her father. Giving the men time to deliberate, she retired to a back administrative room to type up the resolution. When she returned, the document circulated the room. Each leader signed without argument. There was a quiet calm in the room. Dietrich stepped quietly out to call and arrange the meeting. Upon his return, Toriana asked what was said.

"Well" he replied, "They agreed to the meeting. It is going to be at the Krams place, so we can pick up the other girls on the way out."

"Do they know that the huntresses are here?" Toriana asked.

"Not as far as I can tell," he said "but they are still looking for you all."

Toriana went outside to let Lisa know what was going on. Upon hearing the news of the resolution, Lisa wrapped Toriana in a thankful embrace. Toriana felt Lisa's tears of joy against her cheek. As the women pulled away from each other, Lisa wiped her eyes and simply asked, "When?"

"Very soon. We are just waiting for a few other people to show up," Toriana replied.

As Toriana walked back to the council house, she heard a shriek and peel of laughter. Lisa had told the other women what was happening. Everyone was celebrating.

Soon the others arrived. There were many more men from the Fahrenholz pack, as well as a few augmenters from the Bedburgs. The whole of the group quickly loaded into vehicles and made their way to the Krams property. Toriana expected to be nervous or even fearful. She was not. She had been steeled by her newfound strength.

As they approached the Krams homestead, it was clear that the two patriarchs in question had no idea what was ahead of them. There were but two vehicles in front of the house. Just like their approach to the council house, each vehicle parked and wolves fanned out to guard the exterior.

Toriana, Dietrich, Evan, Frank, Clause, and a handful of huntresses walked inside. Leo and Adrian were frozen in their chairs by the sight in front of them. Their mouths moved but no sound came out. Toriana silently walked forward and dropped the resolution on the table in front of them. They both looked at the paper and back at her.

"This is your last warning. Read it, sign it, and follow it or you are on your own."

Adrian turned to Deitrich, demanding answers.

"What the hell is this? Dietrich, I thought you had better control of this little girl."

Toriana cut him off.

"I would be very careful if I were you. I am a full council member now. The rest of the council and I are in agreement, so you might want to get with the program."

Adrian read through the document quickly and flung it across the table to Leo. Leo read through it carefully and, without bothering to look at Adrian, signed it. Frank, who was standing beside Adrian to ensure he didn't become aggressive, looked at him and said, "I guess its just you now."

Adrian began to grit his teeth and scowl. His hands became tight fists and his back arched, all a foreshadowing of a shift. Recognizing this, the huntresses moved in and began their processes as well. Seeing he was outmatched, Adrian released the shift, slumped forward and begrudgingly signed the document. After giving his signature, Adrian pushed the document to the front of the table where Toriana picked it up.

"Thank you. We will leave you two alone now. It would seem that you have a lot to talk about."

The crowd turned and walked outside. Once near their vehicles, Evan turned to Toriana and asked, "What now?"

"Now we go get the rest of them," she replied.

They made their way to the huntress lair. Inside they found the remaining huntresses, frightened and bracing for the worst. Several immediately ran to Toriana, assuming she had been caught and tortured. Seeing that she was intact, one asked, "What is going on?"

Toriana looked at her and smiled.

"Its over. You are free."

The girl burst into tears, as did the others who were standing around. One woman sobbed heavily from grief instead of joy. Lisa went to her and asked her what was wrong. Between sobs the woman said, "Our families don't want us. Where will we go now?"

Lisa looked back at Toriana. She had considered this question but had never asked it. Toriana spoke, addressing the crowd.

"You are all welcome into my pack. We will make a place for you. We are family now."

The women hugged each other and jumped up and down like children. Taking advantage of a moment where everyone's attention was not on Toriana, Evan took her in his arms.

"Are you going to make a place for me too?"

She smiled.

"Its a new world now, Evan. You are my place."

### *The End*

\*\*\*\*\*

Made in United States
Troutdale, OR
01/30/2024